BAT GIRL

The story of those left behind after a horrific crime.

CHAPTER 1

Robert

It was Friday. For most people on the bus that was a cause for celebration. The end of the working week and time to relax with their family and friends. It filled Robert with dread. He twiddled and turned his skull wedding band, pressing the sharp edges into his skin. He grabbed the back of his dreadlocks and pulled them tight. The pink hairband he wore each day was his protection, his talisman. It held no power after 6pm on a Friday.

A small, brightly coloured ball rolled down the aisle and his stomach clenched. He pulled his camouflage jacket firmly around him and hunched in his seat. The ball came to a stop next to him and he heard the clattering of excited feet running down the bus. He mustn't turn round and look. Instead, he stared at the back of the driver's head. The greasy, lank hair that sat just above his jacket collar. Robert shuddered and involuntarily turned away, coming face to face with the child as it knelt down to pick up the ball. He sighed. Only then realising he had been holding his breath. It was a boy, with short black hair and wide brown, heavily lashed eyes. The boy looked nothing like Charly. He could relax as he forced a smile.

CHAPTER 2

Robert

Arriving home an hour later, Robert half expected to see Charly running up the path to greet him. She would hug his legs and he'd ruffle her hair. She always did that when he'd taken the bus. The journey was long and tedious, involving a change at the bus station. The connection often late. Why did all buses have to go through the centre of town? Why couldn't they go around the outer edge? It would make his life so much simpler. Or he could go back to using his motorbike, his pride and joy, but it held no pleasure now. Truth was, he would rather face the drudgery of the bus ride. It meant spending less time in his soulless home.

When he entered the living room, Robert wasn't surprised to see Emma scrolling through, what he assumed was, Facebook on her iPad. He noticed her smile when she read something that pleased her. The parent support group she spent most of her time on helped her to make sense of the loss. How, he did not know. She looked up briefly to acknowledge his presence. There was a pint of green algae, half finished, in a glass on the table next to her. She was beginning to get herself back, while he felt himself diminishing.

'Do you want something edible to go with that?' he asked, pointing at the glass.

'What do you have in mind?' she muttered, squinting at him.

'I was thinking of a Chinese. It's been ages...'

He stopped speaking when he noticed her screw

her face up. This was the first month since Charly's death that Emma had been eating properly.

Of course, Charly hadn't died. She had been murdered, killed, butchered. The headlines were clear. But even when printed in black and white, the facts were still unrepeatable in public. *I hear your daughter died.* You don't correct them. *No, she was butchered by a psychopath.* That would be impolite.

'It's ok,' Robert said evenly, opening the fridge and gripping on to its side. 'How about the rest of the quiche and salad?'

Emma smiled. 'Thanks, that would be nice.'

A chow mein would have been nicer, he thought. It might fill the gap. The emptiness.

Ordering a takeaway on a Friday night. It's what normal couples did. Robert doubted they'd ever be that again.

As he reached for the lettuce, he noticed the dried blood on his finger. It had bled from the pressure of his ring. He lifted his finger to his mouth and sucked. Then he reached back in the fridge for the lettuce.

'You're still wearing it then.' Emma was behind him. She rested her head on his long hair and wrapped her thin arms around his waist. He knew she had always loved the citrus waxiness of his dreadlocks and the way they tickled her cheek.

He guessed she meant the pink hairband. He had found it, discarded on the ground by the swing some days after Charly was abducted. She was always pulling the bands out preferring her curly, blonde hair to be free. Flying behind her as she ran or rode her bike. The hairbands were for school or visiting old relatives where she felt constrained and expected to conform. But the hairband wearer was not his Bat Girl. His sporty, adventurous, independent daughter.

Charly hated pink too. Pink was the colour of Barbies and tutus. But she had torn so many hairbands from her blonde locks that, on that morning, this was the only colour left in the packet.

Robert usually removed the pink hairband as he

walked up his tarmac drive. He didn't need it at home. It never worked. It didn't keep him safe. It didn't stop him breaking down.

No one mentioned it anymore at work. *The scaffolder with the pink hairband.* Well, they wouldn't, would they? Not now. Everybody in Stanton knew what had happened.

CHAPTER 3

W

One person knew what had happened to Charly more than most, but he was a stranger.

A stranger who, when he scuttled up the street, no one mentioned his name. He wasn't the subject of gossip or neighbourly chat. Wearing his hoodie and cap, he could be a local teenager or a regular guy down the pub. Nondescript, average, nothing special.

The stranger sat at the table tapping his knife. Tap pause, tap, tap, tap, pause, tap, tap. An irregular rhythm, but he wasn't bothered by it. He was bored. Bored of being out of sight. Bored of being the last person people noticed. The one who never got the girl. Never captained the football team. Never got chosen as the employee of the month. A nobody. But he was, of course, a somebody.

He felt it welling inside. Not anger. More a darkness that usually simmered just off the boil. A growl that was half spoken, half swallowed. His foot began to tap a quick, anxious rhythm against the laminate. The garish laminate that he would never have chosen. Its pink pattern scuffed and worn. His sister had picked it because it matched the tea towels, before she left and took them with her.

He glanced at the headlines in the paper, picked it up off the scratched kitchen table. The reporters always sensationalised events. The act was far less exciting, much more ordinary, like sliding your knife into a tub of margarine. He never really thought about the girls. Never saw their faces, just their beautiful golden hair. He stood up and went to the sink, dropping the butter knife into the water. Then he sat back down at the table and continued to read the paper.

It was after 6pm on a Friday.

CHAPTER 4

DI Chambers

DI James Chambers wanted to say, 'there's been another one'. But that would have been inappropriate. He never understood why they always said it in crime dramas. It was like the victims didn't matter. They were just a number: one, two…another one.

Instead, DI Chambers put the phone down and gathered the team. They would travel in separate cars to the scene. His bag man, DS Khapor, drove, allowing James to concentrate on his own thoughts without having them interrupted by the everyday prattle of his colleagues. DS Khapor had worked with him long enough to know not to speak unless it was relevant to the case. For DI Chambers, conversation was for his own family. It was what he did when he wasn't at work. At home he could talk about the weather, the cost of milk; at work he talked about death, strategies and suspects. Everyone had a job to do. Each officer should know their role in the investigation. He made that clear at every briefing.

His DCI, as Senior Investigating Officer, would join them later, once all the paperwork was complete. DI Chambers was glad he was, as usual, being trusted to run the Murder Investigation Team. While he sat in the passenger seat of the speeding unmarked car, he called Patrice, the Family Liaison Officer. She had supported Robert and Emma Dean for the past six months and still had regular contact with them.

He thought about the Deans. How Robert Dean broke down. The police had interviewed both parents when

Charlotte went missing. They couldn't understand why she was out so late. It was possible the parents had done it, either together or one of them, in a rage. Taken and hidden their daughter. It happened.

Instead, it turned out, Charlotte had been at her grandmother's while her parents were at a gig. She had sneaked out of the house while her grandmother was making tea. She was never allowed to go to the park next to Granny's and certainly not after 6pm on a Friday. It was full of 'weirdos and freaks', drinking cider out of litre bottles and snogging on the swings.

Charlotte, aged six, was a 'bright independent little girl' so the papers said. Just like DI Chambers daughter, she'd always followed her own path. Loved the outdoors, wasn't glued to the television or a tablet. He had learned all this from Granny. Her parents were inconsolable.

Robert had called Charly 'his Bat Girl' over and over. He rocked incessantly and pulled his own hair so much they thought it might come away from the roots. He howled and squealed and cried. Emma Dean sat catatonic. She looked like a china doll, with hair that had been spiked and sprayed green by a naughty child. A doll that could shatter at any time.

DI Chambers hoped he didn't have to see another set of parents. That this was a mistake. A long-lost discarded shoe, not a body. A skeleton, degraded from thousands of years of burial, of an Iron Age man with an axe hole in his head. But it wasn't. It was another one.

CHAPTER 5

Robert

Robert sobbed silently. Emma was asleep beside him, curled up tightly, her back just touching his side. He felt the warmth of her skin. In the half light of the early morning, he looked at the carpet and tried to concentrate on one spot. A coffee stain. He tried to get his breathing in control. He bit into his hand. He had woken from a dream. Not a nightmare. A memory of Charly's last sports day. She had won the egg and spoon by a mile. Beating both boys and girls. Her happiness lit up her face like morning breaking over the top of a mountain. The good dreams were the worst.

There was a loud knocking on the front door. Emma woke startled, her eyes staring at him in the gloom. She shivered. He covered her with the plain, cotton duvet and kissed her gently on the shoulder.

'It's ok. I'll go,' he said softly and rose.

When he opened the door and saw it was Patrice, his legs nearly buckled. She never came to see them this early in the morning.

'What...?' he began to say.

Patrice asked, 'Can I come in?'

Robert opened the door and called up the stairs to Emma. She didn't hear him at first. He was tempted to let her sleep, but an early arrival could only mean one thing. News.

He didn't listen to Patrice for at least three minutes. He sat beside Emma huddled in one corner of the drab, brown leather sofa. Staring at the Family Liaison Officer. She was talking but just in random words...girl...found dead...same place...good they might find clues...

'What!' Robert gasped, sitting upright.

'How can it ever be good?' Emma asked.

'That poor family. I know...' Robert said.

'I'm sorry,' Patrice said. 'I meant they might find clues as to who murdered Charlotte.'

'Charly,' Robert muttered.

'I want to see them. I can help,' Emma said. She had pulled her knees up to her chin and was hugging her legs, rocking.

'See who?' asked Patrice.

Emma pushed her hair out of her eyes. It still stuck out at all angles from her sleep. No longer green or spiky, as it had been when Charly was alive. It was now a dull brown bob. But Robert noticed that she'd recently dip dyed the ends red. She was coming back to herself.

'The parents,' said Emma. 'I can help.'

'That won't be necessary,' said Patrice.

Emma started to cry. Robert wanted to hold her but had forgotten how. If he wrapped her in his arms, she might disintegrate into dust. Instead, he pressed his body deeper into the sofa and stared at the wall. The pictures of a smiling Charly playing football at the park looked back at him.

'Do you want me to stay a while?' asked Patrice.

That was the last thing they wanted. 'Yes,' they both said.

CHAPTER 6

Robert

The calls came through almost immediately. Withheld or unknown numbers. One after another like firecrackers. Robert ignored them. Didn't answer any of them. Not even later, when the calls were labelled Mum or Jack. He'd seen it all before: reporters, friends, even family wanting to know how he felt, wanting to get inside his head to that forbidden, boarded up place. He picked up the pink hairband and bound it round his hair. Pulled it so tight it hurt his scalp.

He walked into the garage. His Suzuki Bandit sat neglected in the corner. Weather-worn from all the winters' riding he'd previously done. Paint peeling from the wheel arches and engine casing. Salt-corroded pipes and scratched seat. He took a pot from a top shelf. He dumped the contents out on his workbench and shuffled through the old screws and rusty nails until he found the hidden keys for his bike.

He was shocked when on the second attempt the bike fired up. Rumbling and purring, he opened up the throttle and it roared. Smoke billowed from the exhaust, he let it tick over for a minute before turning the engine off. His helmet was in the hall on top of the coat stand, above his leather jacket. Should he bother telling Emma where he was going or just sneak off?

When he went back inside Emma was back on Facebook, no doubt listening to her friends in the Mothers of Murdered Children Group telling her how she should respond to the news. He noticed Patrice's shadow just outside the back door.

She was either smoking a cigarette or phoning her boss DI Chambers. He didn't really care which. He picked up the helmet and jacket and left the house.

He rolled the bike out of the garage and on to the drive. Got on her and started her up. Welcoming the throb of the engine between his thighs, not having ridden in four months. Riding after Charly's death seemed pointless and pleasureless. Either the lads picked him up in the van or he got the bus to work. He never really went anywhere else. But he had somewhere he needed to go now.

Turning on to Sutton Road, he remembered the other times he had come here. Before Charly's death: it was a sanctuary. He loved walking through the trees. He reckoned if he had lived in a previous life, he'd have lived in a treehouse in the middle of a forest. Lighting fires with ease and scavenging for food. Since Charly's death, he'd been here once. Forced to by Emma and her mother. He sat in the car looking in the other direction, as they went to lay flowers and notes. The mere smell of the flowers had made him retch, sickly sweet and cloying. He'd wanted to place, on that spot, Charly's Bat Girl doll that he'd bought her from Forbidden Planet, but he couldn't let it go. He hugged it, in the car, facing the other way.

Reaching the scene, he came to a stop. Forgetting to pull in the clutch, he stalled. He wanted to see this. What they do when they find them. How they are treated. Are they kept safe or violated? He just had to know. He walked towards the trees, to the spot where Charly had been found, knowing from the press reports that this was where the other girl would be. He felt nauseous and anxious, but he knew it must be done.

CHAPTER 7

DI Chambers

'Oh no, it can't be,' DI James Chambers mumbled, spotting Robert running towards the cordon.

The Scene of Crimes Officer turned round, dropping the trowel he was using around the tree trunk. 'What's up...?' He started to say, but James had bounded off to the car park just past the first line of trees.

'I want to see her!' Robert was screaming, wrestling with two police officers. Forcing his way past.

'It's not Charly,' James said.

'I know. I'm not stupid. I need to see her. I need to know...'

'You need to know what?'

'What he did to her...and what you do — when you find them.'

'You can't be here. It won't help anybody. Go home to Emma. Go home where you are needed.'

He didn't want Robert to see all the clinical necessities. The scraping of nails, the prodding and probing. The constant flashing of camera bulbs and scientific, lacking in emotion, chatter of technicians.

Despite the firm grasp of the officers, Robert continued to struggle. 'Needed. I'm needed here to make sure she's safe. For her father, he can't do it. I need to. To give her some dignity.'

Dignity — there was no dignity in violent death.

Robert sank to his knees, still staring at the crisp,

white tent. James looked the other way as Robert began to shake. He hated seeing the outpouring of grief. It was understandable, but it should be a private act. Not for public consumption.

'You need to go home.' James said, putting his hand on Robert's back.

CHAPTER 8

Emma

Emma stared at the television screen. They kept showing the two girls photographs together, side by side, like they were friends. Charly looked so much older than Samantha. Older and stronger. Definitely taller. Maybe she had fought more than Samantha?

She couldn't think like that. Couldn't think about how Charly died. Maybe she should turn off the television or at least switch the channel from the BBC News. For some reason, it helped watching it over and over again. She'd even started counting the minutes between reports. If these grew, as other news stories took over, then that would mean that the girls' deaths were now less important. She dreaded that.

Patrice entered the room. 'Can I get you anything? A cup of tea? Something to eat.'

Emma didn't answer, her eyes transfixed on the television. Worried that If she moved away the girls would be forgotten. They wouldn't have existed. Sitting so close, her mother would have scolded her. "You'll get square eyes sitting there". What did that matter, in the scheme of things?

Half an hour later, Emma heard the front door slam and the sound of a motorbike engine. She didn't stand, didn't go to the window, didn't care to look. They were new videos to watch. Of the poor girl's father. Asking to be left alone.

Emma remembered them. Reporters clamouring, trampling the lawn, bulbs flashing through the net curtains. No decency, no manners. Robert's father screaming at them to leave.

Patrice took control in the end. Ordered them off the premises.

The Porters must have a Patrice. Taking control. Asking unanswerable questions. Blaming. Did you not know where she was at precisely that time? Judging you. Assessing. *I'm here to support you.* Never quite sure if that was true.

Where had Robert gone? Why did he take the bike?

There was the photograph of Charly again. Smiling. Not a care in the world. Emma touched the screen. Stroked her golden hair. No tears.

Emma could see Patrice's reflection, hovering behind her. in the television screen. 'You really should eat. Shall I make you some toast?'

Emma didn't answer. The screen hypnotised her.

Patrice disappeared. Left her to it. Probably bored. The pictures of Charly and the other girl, Samantha ended. They were replaced by a weather report. At the bottom of the screen it said: *a second six-year-old child murdered in Stanton.* There were other less important headlines concerning a bomb in an Iraqi market place. Scrolling along the bottom of the screen. Repeated.

Emma realised their daughter would always be the first murdered six-year-old child. In any reports, she would come first, followed by Samantha Porter, followed by...*no, there wouldn't be more. She couldn't imagine there would be more.*

She heard Robert's bike pull up outside. Didn't move. The news was returning to the scene. The wood. A reporter was speaking to the camera, microphone in hand, 'This is the spot where a second body of a child was discovered early this morning...'

She saw Robert's reflection in the television screen. He was staring at the picture of Charly. Emma touched the screen again. She wanted Robert to move, she couldn't see her daughter properly.

CHAPTER 9

Robert

Patrice opened the front door when Robert pulled up outside his house. Not stalling this time. He wondered how he'd got back safe. He'd ridden aggressively, which he'd never normally do. Taking corners too fast, leaning too far, like a racer, dragging his knee on the tarmac. Not concerned if it left a graze through his unpadded jeans. He thought his boy racer days had long gone. He had a father's responsibilities until six months ago. Today, he didn't care.

He un-flattened his hair as he guiltily walked to the front door. He knew he wasn't a prisoner, but he should have told Patrice where he was going. When she had first arrived at their house as a Family Liaison Officer, he hadn't been sure what her role was. He was concerned that she was sent to spy on them. He felt that DI Chambers hadn't believed that they had nothing to do with Charly's death. It was only when all alibis were checked that everyone's demeanour, including Patrice's changed. Then she was far more comforting, but he still wondered if her role was more to keep them away from the investigation rather than to keep them informed about it.

'I'm sorry if I got you into trouble,' he said, like an errant schoolboy.

Patrice didn't respond as she led him back into the house.

Emma was watching the news. They were showing that picture of Charly, the one they didn't like. The school one. She was smiling but not in a natural way. For the first time, he noticed the glint of pink. She had her hair pulled into a ponytail and he could just see the pink hairband that held it tight.

'She's been watching the news on a loop all morning,' Patrice said.

Robert turned away from the screen. 'I need to talk to you,' he said.

CHAPTER 10

Patrice

Robert followed Patrice into the kitchen and they both sat down at the counter. She noted the anguish etched into his face. The lines of concern. Not just for himself, but for the other grieving father. It was rare for there to be a second murder and she had never considered how it would affect the parents she supported. Emma had become more immersed in the pool of grief; Robert had become more animated, wanting to be involved. To have a role to play. Patrice had a nagging concern that this could cause her problems.

Robert spoke, 'I just need to know what happened to Charly. I've never asked before, but I need to know for his sake.'

'Whose sake?' Patrice asked.

'His, the other father. He'll want to know and, like me, won't be able to ask. I need to know what happens.'

'You want to know how she died?'

'No, not that,' Robert let out a low moan. 'I want to know what you do at the scene. I want to know if you look after her...care for her...I want to know why you keep her there, out in the cold for so long. I need to know.'

What could she say? She understood this desire. At the time of Charly's death, Robert and Emma were all consumed by grief. They wouldn't have given a thought to what was happening to their daughter's body. Patrice, Emma's mother and Robert's parents had done all they could to shield them from the media. But she understood why he would want to know

now. You only had to see a white tent to imagine a body beneath it. The tent was there for a reason. The reality of body retrieval was far more clinical and gruesome than they portrayed in television dramas. The smell. It was the smell that defied description. But Patrice could describe the rest, if it helped.

'I see. Well...there are two things that are important — the scene and the body,' Patrice paused, uncomfortable that she had referred to his daughter as a body. 'We have to be careful that any evidence found is not contaminated, not added to, by what we bring to the scene on our clothes or shoes. The uniformed police arrive first. They tape everything off. In Charly's case this was from behind the tree where they found her, right up to the car park. They have to account for everyone coming in and out...Is this what you wanted to hear?'

'Yes. Exactly. Keep going.' Robert's leg was tapping against the cabinet.

Patrice wondered how much she could and should say. There was a fine line between offering comfort and causing distress; between what a parent needs to know and what an officer cannot disclose. She decided to stick with the procedural facts. 'Anyone that enters the scene has to be white suited and booted. They wear double gloves, a face mask, a white suit and white slip on boots. They should all wear a hairnet but not everyone does. DI Chambers does. He's quite meticulous. They look for the obvious first without moving or touching anything. You can learn a lot this way. Sometimes there is something so obvious and specific that it stands out immediately...' Patrice stopped. Concerned, she might say it out loud.

Robert noticed her pause. 'What was it?'

'There was something. I can't tell you. It's key. A statement. A signature.'

Robert stood up. Paced the floor. 'What was it?' he shouted. He punched the kitchen wall.

'They looked after her. I promise. They cared for her. They didn't do anything that wasn't necessary. DI Chambers will have thought of his daughter and the photographer, his niece. They were careful, respectful, I assure you.'

Patrice stopped speaking. She tried not to think about the photographs she had seen of Charly. Not the ones on the living wall room wall, of her smiling with her beautiful, blonde flowing hair, but the ones after. He had shaved them. Both of them. Removed their hair. Practically scalped them.

'You understand, don't you. Why I can't tell you. When we get him...'

'If you get him.' Robert slammed his hand on the worktop.

'When we get him. It will be the key.'

CHAPTER 11

W

He'd slept in. Something he rarely did. No work today, but he usually spent Saturday gardening. Tiredness consumed him, having spent the night reliving it. Every small part. He wasn't a lingerer. Never wasting time with them. There was no torture involved. Quick, simple, done. One set of tools buried and another to buy.

He woke up recalling the hair removal. Lay with his hands behind his head, staring at the ceiling. Remembering his previous night's work. Being careful that every blonde strand was collected. All important, all special, no matter how fine. Cutting with scissors first right up to the root and clutching the precious locks in his hand. Then with the sharpest razor, shaving right up to the scalp. Each precious blonde hair falling onto the plastic sheet below.

CHAPTER 12

Robert

Monday finally arrived, and Robert prepared for work. Jack, his boss, had told him to take the week, but he didn't want to. He wanted to work. Jack could remember what happened last time. How reporters had followed them around to each job. He'd told Robert that this time he could work in the back office with Mariam and sort the invoices. But Robert refused. He liked been up the scaffold. He liked been exhausted and sweaty and bruised. He, also, needed to be away from Emma and the news on a loop.

Two hours later and he was up top. Fixing the last boards. He glanced over towards Drapers and saw them. All lined up outside a house. A row of them with cameras, like vultures, all dressed in black. He slid down the ladder and ran.

It was hard to work out whose garden was theirs from the back. There was an entry further up, so he jogged up to it and peered round the corner. From this angle, the house appeared to be three doors down. He walked up to the correct gate and found it firmly bolted. He climbed over it and dropped to the floor. The garden was long and wide. Mostly lawned, except for a few flowering shrubs and the odd clump of ground coverers. There was a wooden Wendy House and various toys and bikes littered the lawn.

Purposefully, he walked up to the french doors and knocked. He noticed there were two young boys playing on the rug. One was constantly looking around, checking his surroundings, while the other was engrossed in playing with the Lego. A tall, thin man with wavy brown hair opened the door.

'How did you get in the garden?' he asked.

'I'm sorry. I climbed over the gate. I'm not a reporter.'

'I know who you are,' the man said.

He opened the door fully and Robert stepped in.

'You probably don't remember. You put some scaffolding up for us when we had the windows done. My wife took a shine to your dreadlocks. She's always liked them.'

'I'm Robert Dean,' he offered his hand.

The other man shook it, 'Simon Porter.'

'My daughter was Charlotte — Charly Dean.'

Robert then realised he didn't know what Simon's daughter's name was. He couldn't bear watching the news.

'My daughter's name is Samantha — Sam.' As if reading his mind.

Now he'd got here, he didn't know what to say. He thought it would be easy. He knew what not to say, the things that people said out of kindness, the things that actually really hurt.

Simon started speaking, emotionless, staring outside. 'She was taken from next door's garden. It was sometime after 6:30pm. She'd sneaked through the gap in the fence to feed the rabbits. We didn't know she had gone. Jane thought she'd taken herself up to bed. She did that when she was tired. We'd had a busy day.'

'We didn't protect them. We failed.' There Robert had said it. Out loud. The one thing he'd been thinking and hadn't spoken. But then he'd said very little about that night.

Without looking at Robert, Simon said, 'That's right. We didn't protect them.'

Robert realised that he hadn't come here to help this man. This stranger. He'd come here for himself. He felt out of place.

'Here,' he said. 'Here's my number.' He wrote it on the back of a receipt that he found in his pocket with the 'quote' pen he always carried. 'If you ever need anything. Have any questions. Just want to talk. Or your wife...Emma can help.'

Simon took the receipt and Robert left the kitchen. Looking back through the patio doors, he saw Simon put the receipt in his back pocket. Robert doubted he'd ever hear from him again. He smiled as he watched Simon's older son hug his father's legs. The other child just carried on playing. Oblivious. *Simon was lucky to have other children, they might numb the pain.*

CHAPTER 13

DI Chambers

James stared at the board in front of him. At the pictures of the two girls. The nice pictures not the other ones. He'd covered those with a tea towel, not wanting to upset the cleaners. There were obvious similarities. The same long blonde hair, same vivid blue eyes. Charlotte had a rounder face, she was much taller than Samantha. Samantha had freckles, hundreds of them and a missing front tooth. She had a giggly smile while Charlotte's was wider and crinkled her eyes. They were both the same age, six, but Charlotte seemed older somehow. It was the hair though. Nothing else would have been important.

On his desk sat a yellow notepad and various other items of stationary in their assigned space. Before taking a sharpened pencil out of the pot, he paused, head in hands. This was his fault. A second murder. He should have caught the killer. Seen the patterns, found the evidence. Glancing back at the photos of the smiling girls, he promised them that he'd try harder.

He drew a line down the middle of a fresh, clean page. The tip of the pencil breaking off as he did so. He reached for another. Wrote similarities and differences in capitals at the top of each section. Scribbled notes. He worked alone in his office. He'd told the team to have a night off, at home. Although, he knew they would have gone to the pub first, for a much needed drink. They'd worked solidly since Friday night. Gathering information. CCTV near the forest. Door to door across Drapers. Interviewing the parents. Gathering clues from the scene. All of it bagged and typed. Added to the board. Added to folders on the computers marked with each child's name. DI Chambers preferred to write with a pencil on yellow lined paper. He wrote in capitals on a clean page: *What does he want with the hair?*

CHAPTER 14

Robert

When Robert arrived home after visiting their house: the Porters, Emma was lying on the sofa asleep. He turned off the television and pulled the throw up to her chin and ran his hand through her hair. It felt soft, freshly washed. He decided he actually liked the red tips. They suited this older Emma.

She stirred and opened her eyes looking directly at him. 'Where have you been?' She asked, rubbing her eyes. 'Jack called. He said you walked off site.'

'I found their house by accident, I went there and then walked home.'

'Their house? Whose? The Porters?' Emma sat up.

'Yes.'

'Did you tell them I want to help?'

'I gave Simon my number. I didn't see his wife. I assumed she was upstairs. Sedated.'

Just like Emma had been for weeks after Charly's death. Months really.

He moved closer to Emma. Held her. First time in ages. She rested her head against his chest. He remembered her telling him the statistic. The one about how many couples stayed together after the death of a child. How it was even lower after a murder. He hoped the Porters would. He wasn't sure how he and Emma had managed to. Maybe it was because Emma talked and talked, and he had just listened. Until she found The Group and then she talked to them. That was easier, in a way, they just stopped talking and listening altogether.

CHAPTER 15

W

Two years ago, the stranger had taken up wig making. He read a book from the library hoping it would be easy. He hoped he would just need to buy a few wig making tools. Then, carefully following the book's advice, learn the simple steps to make a wig from freshly, shorn hair.

But it hadn't been simple. In the end after, unsuccessfully, trying to follow the instructions in the book and using many 'how to' videos that he had found on You Tube, he had decided that he needed proper tuition. Within a few months of starting a course at the F.E. College in the next town, he acquired the necessary skills to make a passable wig. He could now single knot hair neatly into the silk net foundation. He would rather take time to do this than use the unsightlier double knots.

It had taken him months to complete a quarter of the wig. He had wasted a great deal of hair just to get it to knot firmly in place and sit in a perfect row. Now he had more, he could continue his task. He smiled and hummed a few lines from his favourite song, Unfinished Sympathy by Massive Attack.

CHAPTER 16

Emma

They made love last night. The first time since Charly died. They'd had sex before, but it wasn't making love. It was too desperate. Too remote. Eyes shut — could have been anybody sex. She loved Robert and had missed him.

They'd met at a New Model Army gig ten years ago. He was in the mosh pit, with his shirt off. She was at the front getting crushed against the barriers. Staring at Justin Sullivan. Listening to every single word. Singing some of them softly. Raising her hands in the air. Dancing as much as space would allow. The words to Green and Grey floating above them, swirling in their heads.

He'd thumped her! Hard! In the back!

When she turned round. He started apologising. She put her finger on his lips and kissed him. The rest, as they say...

Emma thought about this curled up, in Robert's arms, and smiled. Then she remembered Charly and stopped.

She got up. Put her slippers and dressing gown on, picked up her iPhone and went downstairs. Rachel was online. She was angry. Cross that her own mum had been to the papers again. Emma hated the anger, flicked through it, couldn't cope with it. She only liked the cheery posts. The 'I've survived another day' posts. Or the ones that described the good times. The trips to the park, the holidays, the school plays. Happy memories. She'd done anger.

She made tea and toast. Breakfast in bed. It was

early, but she didn't know if Robert was going back to work today. She knew Jack didn't want him to. He'd told her last night when he rang to say Robert had gone missing. She was pleased, in a way, that he'd gone to see the other family but wished she had gone too.

She wanted to go back to work full time. Instead she was still doing odd hours in the bookshop. Until recently just sorting the orders coming in, out of sight, in the back room. Over the last couple of weeks, she'd started serving more customers. No one seemed to recognise her and she realised, this was because, she had changed. Her hair, the way she dressed, even her size — gone from a 10 to a 6 then back up to an 8. She'd become a vegetarian, although Robert hadn't noticed, and started eating healthily and drinking 'miracle' juices.

Robert was awake when she got upstairs. He actually smiled when she passed him his tea.

'I'm not going in today. Do you fancy a walk?' he said.

CHAPTER 17

Emma

So there Emma was, holding on tight, on the back of the Bandit. It was stop, start. Never filter on this road. Too many side streets. Too many BMW drivers never using their indicators, pulling out without a care or a thought. Then out into the countryside. Tight corners and turns. Racing past tractors and Minis. Singing in your helmet and flying through the wind. Then slowing — slipping down into first, turning. Stopping at the edge of the forest.

They'd come at it from the back way not the car park. She got off the bike, took off her helmet and stared at Robert. 'Why are we here?' she said.

'We can get in this way.'

He took her hand, like last night. The palm felt warm and soft. She wrapped her fingers round his calloused and broken knuckles.

She felt uneasy. She remembered her eighteenth birthday. She'd had a massive row with her then current boyfriend. It was nine o'clock. It was the middle of winter and pitch black and he wanted her to walk through the woods to the park. She'd wondered if he was going to hurt her. In the woods, just the two of them. Then suddenly, as they left the woods and stood on the path, all of her friends jumped out. They'd bought fireworks — which she hated — it was a surprise for her birthday. She remembered they broke up soon after. She'd never forgot the apprehension though.

Robert took her deeper into the woods.

CHAPTER 18

Robert

The trees were getting denser and the ground was getting thicker with stumps, bracken and ferns. People didn't normally use this route. He stopped.

He looked at Emma's ashen white face. 'Just a minute, I'm not sure where we are,' he said.

He let go of her hand. She moved closer towards him and lay her head on his chest, pulling him closer to her. He could hear her heartbeat loud and fast.

'Why have we come here?' she asked.

He held on to her. He didn't want to lose what they had last night. He remembered how beautiful, soft and amazing she was. How she completed him and had made him whole for those few hours. He didn't know why he'd brought her here. The only reason he could think of was that he didn't want to lose her again, so being apart today was just not an option.

'He bought Charly here,' Robert whispered. 'I want to know why?'

He. Emma and Robert had never spoken about Him. Never said a word.

Robert took hold of Emma's hand and started walking again. The route was getting clearer and he thought he saw light blinking through the trees. They were getting closer to the edge of the forest. Maybe, the right edge.

Five minutes later, they reached a line of police tape. Robert touched it. Rubbed his fingers along it. It was part of their story now. Charly and Samantha's. Part of their life was a strip of police tape, saying *keep out, do not contaminate me.* The police seemed to have left. Finished with the scene. Robert noticed a break in the tape further along. He pulled Emma in that direction.

It wasn't long before they reached the tree. Robert recognised it straight away. He just knew it was this tree. It faced the car park. Slightly hidden by a row of bushes. But it would have clearly displayed them. The side of the bark was hollowed out like a seat and this is where He placed them. He wanted them found quickly.

Robert realised he'd climbed this tree thousands of times as a child. It was one of those trees with a long thick set of branches low enough to the ground to set you off. He placed his foot in the well and started to climb. He looked down and saw Emma wince, as though he'd somehow consecrated Charly's grave. He just had a feeling that this climb was essential. So much more important than anything else.

He could climb much more easily than when he was ten. It took him seconds to reach the branches he needed to. He tested their weight and turned to look over Stanton. He spotted Charly's Primary School at the top of the hill. It was break time and he could see the faint blobs of tiny heads. If only he had binoculars.

If he looked to the right, he could see Drapers. The area where professionals lived. When he was younger, he dreamed of owning a house there that had a long garden, where he could plant, grow and tender saplings. He realised that the neat row of gardens that he was looking at included Sam's house. He saw the wooden Wendy House. He imagined Sam playing with her dolls and pushchair.

This wasn't merely the dumping ground. This was where He stalked them. His daughter and Sam. He sat here in this tree and watched them.

'We need to go to see DI Chambers,' Robert shouted down to Emma, who was staring up, through the branches shielding her eyes.

CHAPTER 19

W

The wig maker stroked the blonde locks on the table in front of him. Flattening them out. He reached for a comb and gently separated each strand. The partially constructed wig was already placed on the block. He then attached the blonde wavy hair to the drawing mat ready to begin. Next to the mat, he lined up each of the tools that he needed. Wiping them one by one with a tea towel until they shined. He paused for a moment and smiled. The pleasure he got from weaving the wig would one day be surpassed by having her wear it.

CHAPTER 20

DI Chambers

DI Chambers sat in his office facing Emma and Robert. He wasn't sure what they wanted. Why they had been brought to his office by the front desk. He hadn't even had time to cover the board in the next room. He furrowed his brow and hoped one of the team had the sense to do it.

Robert clenched his hands together. 'He stalks them,' he said.

James and the team had already realised this. Months ago, when Charly was killed. He guessed that Charly wasn't randomly taken, after 6pm on a Friday, from a park usually frequented by skaters and emos drinking cheap cider.

'What makes you think that?' James asked.

Robert told him about the tree. He described in detail what he could see. Stammering as he mentioned the school and the tiny black dots of children playing. Theorising that the killer would have binoculars and could have clearly seen his daughter playing a game with her friends. Perhaps running from one side of the playground to the other. He looked so uncomfortable as he spoke. Each sentence made him visibly shudder and squirm in his chair. The realisation that his daughter was chosen out of a school of two hundred children.

As Robert spoke, James put aside his assumptions. Saw past the father's grief and discomfort. Honed in on what was important. He made a mental note to reprimand the uniformed officer that should have been guarding the area. When he'd finished speaking, James was quick to dismiss them. Eager for them to leave the office and go home, so he could check. Send one of the younger men or women up the tree.

CHAPTER 21

Emma

On Saturday morning, Emma was getting ready to go food shopping. She was searching for her keys when the doorbell rang. She answered the door expecting it to be one of her neighbours. They seemed to be doing a relay on checking if they were okay and offering to cook them a meal. Emma suspected that what they were really doing was fishing for a piece of gossip they could share between them. It wasn't like any of the neighbours normally spoke to them. Nearly all of them were families, with small children, who kept themselves to themselves. Emma wasn't sure why after a second murder that they had all come out of the woodwork. Maybe it wasn't so close to them this time. Emma usually just shooed them away with a "thanks, but no thanks".

It wasn't a neighbour. It was Patrice. 'Can I come in? Is Robert here?'

'He's in the shower,' Emma blushed. It was 11 o'clock. Robert was just getting up. She had been up since six thirty and had cleaned the house from top to bottom.

'Pop the kettle on then and we can have a cup of tea while we wait for him.' Patrice sat herself down on her usual chair.

Emma decided that there was little point protesting, the shopping would have to wait. Patrice wouldn't get any biscuits though. They'd run out. In fact, there was barely any milk left.

'I just need to go next door. I won't be a minute,' Emma shouted from the kitchen. Might as well make some use of the neighbours.

Jim, a mechanic, lived next door. His wife and kids were "away at her mother's". They'd been away a few weeks now. Hopefully, he could lend them some milk.

Emma knocked his door. Jim answered it in his dressing gown. 'Sorry just got out the shower.'

He wasn't wet, Emma noticed. 'You couldn't borrow us a cup of milk, could you? I was just about to go shopping and we've had a visitor.'

Jim ushered her in. 'Yeah, course. It's that Family Liaison woman, isn't it? Everything okay?'

Emma winced. Jim continued, 'Sorry, stupid thing to say. It must bring everything back…you know.'

'Yes. But Patrice thinks it might help. They might have a better chance of catching him.'

'I bloody hope so, Emma.' Jim reached into the fridge and took out a litre plastic bottle of semi-skinned. 'My wife and kids might come back if they do.'

'Oh.' Emma looked at the floor.

'It's not your fault, love. Any bloody excuse really. We weren't exactly getting on.'

Emma had heard the rows, but never said anything. Well, you don't.

'Here, have all of this.' Jim thrust the bottle at her, 'I've got to go to Asda later anyway.'

'Thanks, but a mug full will do.'

'This is easier to carry. You might as well have it. I'll never finish it on my own.'

Emma was glad to leave. She found it impossible these days to show others any kind of sympathy. She couldn't find the words.

By the time she got back to her house, Robert was up and dressed. He followed her into the kitchen and watched her make the tea. 'What does Patrice want? Has she said?'

'No, we were waiting for you.' Emma didn't hide her annoyance that he'd stayed in bed so long.

''I've been at work all week, okay,' Robert scowled.

'I wasn't complaining. Just stating a fact.'

The tea was ready. Emma gave Robert a mug and then took Patrice's into the living room. 'Here you go. There's no biscuits or anything. Sorry.'

Patrice smiled. 'That's fine.'

'Why are you here?' Robert was still scowling. Emma gave him a look.

'The Porters are going to do a television appeal. We thought you might want to join them.' Patrice slurped her tea.

Emma waited for Robert to respond. He didn't.

'I know you didn't want to do it last time.' They couldn't. They could barely speak. Emma didn't need to be reminded.

'Can we think about it and get back to you?' Robert eventually said.

'It will have to be today. We need everything set up for Monday lunchtime to catch the news.' Patrice paused. 'I know it's hard, but it might jog someone's memory. Even now.'

They hadn't got any witnesses. Not to Charly's abduction. Not one. Despite the fact, at that time on a Friday night, they were probably teenagers hanging out at the park.

Patrice was still talking, Emma had tuned out. 'The Porters might appreciate the support too.'

Her ears pricked up at this. 'We could help them, you mean? We had nobody but you're right we could support them. Robert?'

Robert was still angry. Emma wasn't sure why. 'You can do it if you want. I don't know…' He got up then and went to the kitchen.

'I'm sorry, I don't know what's up with him,' Emma apologised.

'It's okay, I know this is hard,' Patrice said. 'For both of you.'

'I'll talk to him. Get back to you later.'

Patrice finished her tea and stood to leave. 'Thanks. That would be great.'

'I wouldn't know what to say.' Emma followed Patrice to

the door.

'We'll help you with that, don't worry. It would be good if you could do it. Good for the investigation.'

'I'll talk to him.' Emma nodded her head towards the kitchen.

'Thanks.' Patrice touched Emma's arm and then walked down the path towards her car.

Robert had come back to the living room. He sat on the sofa with his head in his hands.

Emma sat next to him and put her arm round him. 'We should do the appeal.'

'Look at us, Emma. We're freaks. That's what people will think. They'll look at the Porters in their smart clothes. Then they'll look at us with my dreads and your dyed hair. They'll sympathise with the Porters and just think, look at those freaks — they don't deserve to be parents.'

CHAPTER 22

Emma

Emma wasn't sure what she'd said to convince Robert but here they were sitting in the Britannia Hotel, waiting to be told that it was time to start the appeal. Simon Porter was sitting in a chair at the other side of the foyer. Jane wasn't with him. Emma didn't blame her for not doing it. It was tough. No one had spoken. Robert kept looking down at his clothes then over at Simon. Comparing.

Simon looked pale and drawn. He wore a grey suit and open necked white shirt. His clothes were immaculate and black shoes, freshly polished. Emma wondered if Jane had washed and ironed, instead of doing the appeal.

She nudged Robert. 'We should go over and say something.'

'I feel sick.' Robert didn't look sick. Not like Simon who looked as if he could vomit at any time.

'It's just nerves.' Emma showed Robert her hands. 'Look at me. I'm shaking.'

'You go over if you want. I can't physically get up off this chair.'

Emma glanced over again at Simon. His Family Liaison had joined him. At least Emma thought that's who she was. She was speaking animatedly to Simon waving her arms around as though she was explaining who would be in the room. It was too late to go over now. Simon had someone. Emma wondered where Patrice was. She should be here too.

Robert must have noticed this. 'Someone should be telling us what to expect.'

To be fair, Patrice had spent most of yesterday afternoon going through the questions. She'd even told them what to wear. They had both just nodded at this. Neither of them possessing the items of clothing she was suggesting. Emma looked down at her black jeans and black jumper. She hoped people didn't think that she was still in mourning. It would be considered too long to mourn. Black might not look good for the cameras. But she didn't care if she looked good anyway. Robert looked pretty much the same. He hadn't polished his Doc Martens either. Perhaps he was right. Everyone would think they were freaks.

DS Khapor entered the foyer. He sought them out first. 'We're on in about ten minutes. You can take your seats now.'

Emma needed the toilet but decided it would be better just to get it all out of the way.

They all sat in a line. Simon. Then her and Robert. Then DI Chambers. Then another man that did all the television stuff. He was a DCI and when he started speaking, he introduced himself as the Senior Investigating Officer. Emma couldn't remember meeting him before. Perhaps they weren't important enough.

Robert had a piece of paper in front of him. He was physically shaking. His leg was pressed against hers and it felt like he was doing an Irish jig under the table. Emma took his hand in hers. Bulbs flashed. She shielded her eyes. The room was packed. They were even people standing at the back. She was relieved Robert was going to speak and not her. Emma held his hand tighter.

CHAPTER 23

Robert

Robert couldn't quite believe he was here sitting in front of the vultures. Why was he doing this? Emma took his hand. She squeezed it tight. It was for her. No, it was for Charly. That's what he had to think. He was doing this for Charly. To help find her killer.

Her killer was, no doubt, out there watching. Reveling in the parent's anguish. Or maybe simply not caring. He wouldn't give himself up if Robert asked him to. That's not how it worked.

Patrice had said that they needed to do this to jog people's memory. There might be a witness who hadn't realised that what they had seen was important. Or there might be someone who knows the killer. Has seen them acting suspiciously. Someone who will give them up. Or no one could come forward and the whole thing would be a waste of time.

The self-important police officer had stopped talking and was looking Robert's way, it must be his turn to speak. The microphone was passed down the table like a relay baton, Robert was scared he'd drop it. Emma put it in front of him and then put her hand on his thigh. His leg stopped shaking for a moment. He had a speech typed on A4 paper. He lifted it slightly and his hands shook so he placed it back down on the table and began to speak. 'Our daughter Charly...' He glanced at Emma, who smiled back at him and squeezed his thigh. '...was abducted on Friday 11th November just after six in the evening at Bradstone Park.'

Robert felt the need to explain rather than read the next

part. Explain why she was out at the park at night. Explain so people don't think —. 'She'd sneaked out. She was staying at Em's mum's. It was the first time we'd been out in months. She went to the park because she loved flying high on those swings. She loved being outdoors.' Tears started to form. He coughed and went back to the script. Tried to ignore the errant tears that were now streaming down his face and dripping onto the paper. He couldn't see the words.

Emma took the paper from him and spoke, 'Were you in or near the park that evening? Did you see anything or anyone? Please come forward. We need your help. Charly needs your help. We can't bring her back, but we don't want any more children hurt.'

Robert felt ashamed. He covered his face with his hands. Emma stopped speaking and hugged him. He should have read the whole statement, but he just couldn't.

CHAPTER 24

W

This was mildly amusing. Watching Robert sitting there. Shaking pathetically. Emma looking as beautiful as ever. Had she dyed her hair again? She'd look better as a blonde.

He had decided to make a little snack and treat himself to a beer. Fortunately, he didn't have to work today, and it felt like Christmas. It's not every day you get to witness such fascinating television. This was almost as good as an Attenborough documentary. It was like watching that polar bear sneaking up on the seal pup.

He dunked the Dorito into the salsa dip and took a bite. That arrogant DCI spoke first. He wittered on about witnesses coming forward. As if he'd be stupid enough to be seen. He watched as the DCI ran his hand through his hair, preening for the camera. What an idiot.

They were passing the mike down now. It was like observing a pass the parcel. Please stop on Robert. He mimed some music. Stopped at the right spot, raised his hands and cheered.

Robert was talking about his daughter. Trying to explain why she was alone at night on the swings. He could have thanked Robert for that. He couldn't quite believe it himself. She was like a gift left out for him. A perfect surprise. Swinging up and down. His favourite part was when she got rid of that hairband. Then her blonde hair had flown behind her. Beautiful. He took another swig of beer.

Robert was crying. This was priceless. He started to giggle. Now Emma was speaking. He shut his eyes and listened to her voice. It was soft, imploring. It would do.

CHAPTER 25

Emma

A couple of days later, Emma went to do the weekly shop. She always shopped after work on a Thursday. She used to pick up Charly from school first. Charly loved to run down the aisles, helping her mum, picking up the regular items — the bread, the soup, the beans. They'd carry the bags home between them. Charly never moaned, even though the plastic often cut into her skin. Today, Emma had bought one large 'bag for life' that she now used. Not noticing the weight, there was less to carry.

She was walking through the car park when she spotted her, struggling to get the bags into the car. The trolley had a life of its own and was moving out into the traffic. Emma rushed over to stop it.

'Thank you,' the woman with the long, plaited, golden hair said.

Emma knew it was Jane. She'd seen her in the photographs in the paper. Looking distraught. She was surprised she was out of the house, particularly after not being able to do the television appeal. Maybe, she needed the change, the escape, the route back to normality. Emma recognised the look, the gauntness, the grief.

Jane was staring at Emma. Struggling to place her but knowing she should know her.

'I'm Emma Dean,' was all she needed to say.

The woman shrank, stepping back. She clearly didn't know how to respond.

'Why don't we go for coffee. I can help,' Emma said.

There was a coffee shop attached to the supermarket. They'd recently upgraded the machines to Costa rather than the dishwater they'd previously served. Emma chose a latte and Jane a cappuccino. They went and sat at a table by the window.

So, this was the woman "who liked her husband's dreads". It was strange she looked so ordinary. Not the type that would go for the crusty look at all. The papers said she was an administrator at the hospital and her husband was an accountant. They would never have met or spoken if it wasn't for this.

Jane stared out of the window, then turned to face Emma, picking up her mug, she drank. Emma noticed she had left a line of milk on her top lip and she was not too embarrassed to lick it off, rather than wipe it on a tissue. Emma liked that. Jane had beautiful, slightly freckled skin, thought Emma, like that woman on *Casualty*, the consultant. Emma had always wanted skin like that instead of pale, washed out. But it was her hair that caught your attention. Just like Charly's.

'Do you shop here all the time?' Emma asked for something to say.

'Yes.'

They both shopped here. Emma, because it was closest. Jane, because Waitrose was too expensive for what it is. Two women from opposite sides of the town. Shopping in the same place.

'Sam liked to come with me. She'd run along the aisles. Helping me.' Jane said, tears forming again.

Emma put her hand over Jane's and they sat silently. The sudden realisation. She shivered as she thought, maybe He's here today. Looking for another one.

A few minutes later, Jane stood up in a sudden rush to go. Her husband would be worried. He was with the boys. Grabbing her bag. Emma tried to hug her, but she shied away.

As soon as Emma got home, she texted Patrice, not wanting to bother DI Chambers. He'd been so dismissive before. 'We use the same supermarket. The Porters and us.' It said.

CHAPTER 26

Emma

It was after 6pm on a Friday.

Emma heard the sound of a car engine, looked out of the window and saw her mum's car pull into the drive. She looked for Robert. Whenever her mum, Janice, called round he would disappear upstairs. Never wanting to talk to her. It was as though he blamed her. For Charly. He was in the kitchen making a vegetable soup. He'd already commented on the fact that Emma seemed to have forgotten the meat again. He'd assumed she'd been distracted when she bumped into Jane.

'Mum's here,' she said and went to answer the door. Robert hadn't moved, he was still chopping the carrots.

'Oh love. I've been wanting to come round for days but I didn't want to upset you. I've been waiting for you to call,' Janice said kissing Emma on the cheek. Emma felt a little guilty for not ringing her at all, for weeks.

Janice raised her eyebrows. Robert was still downstairs. She looked torn between talking to him, something she'd barely done in months, or going into the living room. Emma watched as her mum, biting her lip, headed for the kitchen.

'Robert,' she said.

'Janice,' he said and carried on chopping.

Emma stood in the doorway, observing these two people she loved, not knowing how they could resolve the gap between them.

'How are you doing?' Robert asked.

'I've been busy at the charity shop. Since that programme on the elderly in care homes everyone wants to donate. I think they are feeling sorry for us lonely, old women.'

    Mum was only fifty. She liked to milk it. Emma smiled, and Robert laughed. He actually laughed. His blue eyes all scrunched up at the corners, just like Charly's. He was laughing.

CHAPTER 27

DI Chambers

DI Chambers reviewed the results of the TV appeal. Disappointing was the only way to describe them.

The first showing on the lunchtime news had brought the regulars out of the woodwork. John from the nursing home, a prime example. John had met the killer many times. He announced that the killer was one of Stanton's five serial killers that he regularly shared a drink with at the local pub. The killer had described to him in detail both murders and where he had burned the children's blonde hair. He needed it for a pagan ritual that would bring him an endless supply of cash. DC Anne Black had taken the call. James had seen the raised eyebrows and knew straight away who she had at the end of the line. Twenty minutes later and she was still there 'umming' in agreement and taking copious notes.

When they'd spoken about it afterwards. James wondered how he knew about that the hair was important. John was known for picking up on the nuances of individual cases. Maybe it was obvious that the girl's long blonde hair was a factor or maybe he was just a lucky guesser.

Then there was Hilda, the curtain-twitcher. On both the evenings that the children were abducted, she had seen a tall man walking down her street, acting suspiciously. James had picked up this call. He knew how to deal with Hilda officiously and politely. Getting her to stick to the facts. He recorded what she said and within ten minutes ended the call. Best not to offer encouragement in any form.

James would send a couple of Police Constables round to take witness statements. At least they'd get tea and biscuits, maybe even cake.

The evening news produced little in the way of new information.

The news at ten was more fruitful. A harassed sounding mother called to say that her son had been at the park on the night Charly was abducted. He hadn't seen anything important or at least that was what he was telling her, but he had been there. He went to the park every Friday on his skateboard.

The skateboard park was opposite the swings, but it would have been dark by that time. James hoped this wasn't going to turn out to be a waste of time and resources, but he knew he would need to interview the lad.

CHAPTER 28

DI Chambers

DI Chambers had only worked with PC Trent on two previous occasions. Both times he had the annoying habit of interrupting him to ask the most ridiculous questions. PC Trent was young and had only recently passed out from Hendon Police College, but even so.

DI Chambers didn't make conversation in the car. He was annoyed that he'd got to interview a child with a probationer. If both DS Khapor and DC Black were busy they could have at least got him an experienced constable. He'd have a quiet word with the duty sergeant when he got back to the station.

They were nearing the address the skateboarder's mother had provided. 'Just leave all the talking to me. You just take notes.' DI Chambers didn't hide his annoyance.

'But...' PC Trent's eyebrows raised as though he was over excited and just had to tell DI Chambers something important.

'No buts. Just do what I'm telling you. Listen to the questions, you might learn something about interviewing a minor. They can be...tricky.'

PC Trent dropped his shoulders and looked out of the passenger window. 'I think this is the road,' he said, pointing to the left.

'Thanks, I know.' DI Chambers turned into the quiet cul-de-sac and pulled up at the third house on the left.

Ten minutes later, the lad had been called down from his bedroom and both officers had been provided with tea and biscuits.

DI Chambers started the interview. 'Jordan, your mum has told us that you were in Bradstone Park on Friday 11th November, is that correct?'

The lad was sucking on a biscuit and muttered a barely audible, 'Yeah.'

'Jordan this is really important, that poor girl was murdered, love.' Jordan's mum was sitting on the arm of the chair that her son lounged on. She leaned in and ruffled his hair. Jordan leant away from her.

'I didn't see nothing, though.' Jordan spluttered on his biscuit. 'Which is why I never said anything before. I wasn't supposed to be there. So…'

'Why don't you tell us what you did when you got to the park?' One step at a time, DI Chambers thought.

Jordan sighed. 'I was supposed to meet my mate at half five, but he didn't turn up, so I rode around on my board for a bit.'

'Which mate was this?' It was possible he'd come to the park, but they'd missed each other. He would need to check.

'Anthony Smith. He lives on Shelton Road, on the other side of the park.'

'Thanks. I'll get his number off you later.' DI Chambers nodded to PC Trent to get him to make a note and remind him. He would get DS Black to interview Anthony since she was better at interviewing boys off the Estate having grown up there herself. 'So, you arrived at the park, where did you wait for Anthony?'

'By the main entrance. I sat on the wall.'

'The main entrance on Bradstone Road?'

'Yeah, that one.'

'How long did you wait for?' DI Chambers took a sip of the insipid tea, instantly regretting it, but wishing to appear polite.

'About ten minutes. Then I got bored. I texted him, so he knew I'd gone off to the skatepark.' Jordan helped himself to another biscuit just as his mum tried to remove the plate.

'Did you notice any of the people coming into the park before you left?'

'It was quite dark. The lights are sh...rubbish in there.'

DI Chambers noted the look that Jordan got. It was similar to the looks he'd given his own daughter growing up. There was a time to swear and a time to be polite.

'But did you see anyone enter the park. Even a brief description might help?'

'There was a coupla kids my age. They were into each other. If you know what I mean.' Jordan laughed. *Into each other.* DI Chambers took this to mean they were kissing.

He took a description of the couple. No one had come forward as being in the park at that time. It might be worth putting out a specific appeal for them to come forward. Maybe DS Black could contact the local schools and youth clubs.

'Anyone else?'

'Don't think so...Oh yeah, there was some bloke with his hoodie up and cap down. Looked like he was rushing home from work. Didn't see his face though.'

'Describe him to me.'

DI Chambers made a note of the description Jordan gave. It was vague at best but average height, dark hair, white, would eliminate some.

'Did you see this man again? Think carefully before you answer. You were riding around the park...even if it was only from a distance. It might help us place him in the park.'

Jordan sat and chewed his bottom lip.

A few seconds later, he said, 'When I was riding my board up to the skatepark, I felt a bit weird, like someone was watching me.'

DI Chambers knew that senses were often more astute than people gave them credit for. If Jordan felt that someone was watching him then chances are they were. 'What did you do at the skatepark?'

'I just sat at the top of the slope. There was glass all over the bottom of it. Some c... idiot has been drinking there again. So, it was unrideable. So, I just put my headphones on and listened to my music.'

PC Trent interrupted. 'If you were sitting up there then behind you was the swings. That's right, isn't it?'

DI Chambers shot him a look but then he had a point. Unless he'd turned round then he wouldn't have seen what was happening at the swings. They should go and measure, but he estimated the distance between the swings and the skate park as about fifty metres. If Jordan was wearing headphones, then he quite possibly wouldn't have seen or heard anything.

Jordan continued. 'I went to the swings after the skate-park...One of the swings was moving. Swinging back and forth. I had to stop it to get on it.'

The significance of that hung in the air. Swinging back and forth.

CHAPTER 29

w

    He sat patiently knotting each exquisite strand of hair. Careful not to damage it pulling it through the net with the hooked needle. The block was mounted on the dressing table in the spare room. He'd glued it straight on to the surface to prevent it from moving. The curtains were pulled tight across the window, so nobody could see. He worked like this for hours. The timer on his alarm clock set, so he didn't miss work that evening.

CHAPTER 30

DI Chambers

Patrice was angry. James knew she was angry because she'd practically slammed the door off its hinges when she came into his office.

'You can't treat them like this,' she said.

James just stared at her. Not really sure what she meant.

'I know I'm family liaison and it's my job to work with the parents, but you've got to spend time with them too. Dismissing them out of hand when they've got important information to the case is just not good enough.'

Had he? He couldn't really remember. She was still talking; did she never take a breath.

'Look James. You are the best detective I know, and you can talk to suspects for hours. Or rather listen to them and throw in the right question just at the right time. But, seriously, you need to learn to deal with the victim's families.'

Fair enough, he hadn't spent long with Robert Dean when he'd told him about the tree and, yes, he hadn't spoken to the parents at the appeal. So maybe, she had a point. But that was her job really, not his. He couldn't cope with the grief to be honest. He felt for them, but his job was to help the victims. To know the killer.

She was still talking.

'Well now Emma's met Jane and found something out. It's really pivotal. They shopped at the same supermarket. Asda, the one near town. They both regularly took the girls there too.'

James thanked Patrice for this key piece of information. He, also, asked her if it was wise that the two families seemed to be talking so much to each other. He asked her to do something about it. Then he wrote on a new page in his yellow pad: shopped at the same supermarket.

CHAPTER 31

Emma

It was Saturday afternoon and they were still in bed. Emma was staring at Robert. He had his arms over his head, clutching the pillow snoozing. She looked at the fine new hairs at the back of his neck. They were always blonder than the rest. She played with them, twisting them into the roots of his dreads. He turned over, looked at her and smiled.

'We ought to get up. Instead of wasting the whole day,' she said.

'I don't think we've been wasting it. I've had a great time,' Robert said, grinning. Emma gave him that look. The one she did when she was pretending he was being scolded. She placed her hand on his tattooed chest and he took it in his.

'I was thinking. Maybe He works there. At the supermarket. We could go there. Get something for tea. You could get some meat. I don't want any though, I'm sort of off it right now.'

She wasn't sure why she suggested it. It seemed like a good idea. But how would you know what He looked like? Was it even a He? They'd always assumed but...

'Let's get dressed. I'll treat you to a latte,' Robert said.

CHAPTER 32

Emma

They'd sat in the coffee shop at Asda for two hours. They'd bought bags of shopping that they'd probably never eat. Robert had insisted on buying bacon, which Emma was annoyed about but didn't say.

'Maybe it's the guy behind the cheese counter,' Robert said. 'He always stares through you like you're not really there.'

'I know his sister. She comes in the bookshop. It won't be him.'

She stared into the car park. The guy pushing the trolleys around, had his cap pulled tightly over his head. It was raining. He seemed completely preoccupied in getting every last one neatly attached to his line.

There was no one really. No one suspicious. The woman behind the fish counter. She was lovely, always used to talk to Charly about her week. She never spoke to Robert or Emma, just Charly. Since Charly's death, the fish counter woman was always busy when they came into the store. Serving other customers or checking he price tags on the fish. It made Emma love her more. She clearly missed their daughter and didn't know what to say to make things better.

The women on the checkout always seemed too busy to really notice you. Apart from Nadiah, she was great, always commenting on Emma's hair. She liked the same type of music and would let Emma know who was playing locally. Not that she ever went to the gigs, not any more. In fact, she rarely listened to music. But she always made a mental note of what was current and Nadiah's favourite bands. Leaving them to one side, until she was ready to listen again.

There was no one. No one fitting the bill. But what did a killer look like? How would you know if you saw one?

'This is hopeless,' Emma said, 'let's go home.'

CHAPTER 33

Robert

Emma was having a bad day. She'd gone into Charly's room and closed the door. Robert would never go in there. Hadn't since that night. There would be so much to remind him of his daughter still in that room.

No one tells you what the right thing is to do. No one tells you whether you should hide everything away after your child dies or keep it on display as a reminder. There isn't a rule book handed out to grieving parents about how they should react or behave. He was totally led by Emma regarding Charly's room. He knew that every time Emma entered the room, she was in pain and he couldn't stop it.

He didn't know what she did in there, but this time he felt his chest tighten. He went back to bed and pulled the cover over his head, wishing he could help her on days like this.

He closed his eyes tight. Willing himself into an untroubled sleep. Dreams were a constant. Nightmares a battle of wills between memories and the darkest thoughts of death. He pushed them away, but they were always there in the periphery of his mind. Taunting him. *This is how your daughter died.*

Recurring dreams. Playground swing rocking back and forth, no child sitting on it. The pink hairband floating to the ground. Hiding itself, ready to be discovered later by a desperate father.

Robert knew every splintered edge of that swing. He'd sat next to it and cried every night in reality and in his dreams. Watched as he plunged his own hands deep into the bark, discovering softness amongst the shattered edges of the crushed wood. He'd never told the police that he'd found the hairband. Never told Emma that he'd gone to the park every night for a month, while she'd lay in a drug induced sleep unaware that his side of the bed lay empty.

These weren't the worst dreams. They came with a thunderous entrance that made his heart beat so hard in his chest that he couldn't breathe. He'd lie paralysed not even able to move a fingertip. Eyes wide open. The scene playing like the bloodiest horror movie in front of him. Watching the murder of his daughter by a faceless monster. The blade flashing, plunging repeatedly into her flesh. He'd wake to the sounds of his own screaming. One night even vomiting with the horror of it.

CHAPTER 34

Emma

Emma lay on the bed in Charly's room and sobbed. She could do this here. Knowing that Robert wouldn't see her. It was a place he never entered. Too many memories. She could come here and hide away. Shut the door on the world.

Some days she came here to talk to Charly. To tell her about her day. The strange people that came into the shop and their odd choices of books.

Some days she came to read to Charly. The latest new children's book with its beautiful unspoiled pages. She read aloud and showed her each picture. She spoke in numerous voices for all of the characters: the loud bossy ones, the quiet ones, the scatty ones, the posh ones, the cackling witches and the wise old owls, each with their own rhythm and tone.

Some days she played with the Playmobil left out on the desk. The small doctors, nurses and patients in the hospital with their various diseases and complaints. She told Charly all their stories, encouraged her to join in.

She had stripped the room three times and put everything in labelled boxes. Only to, hours later, put everything back where it was.

Today she just sobbed until there was nothing left. Then she lay staring at the wall. The spot where Charly had peeled back the wallpaper when she was three and didn't know any better.

CHAPTER 35

Robert

Emma must have climbed into their bed sometime in the night. When Robert awoke she was snuggled up against him. She'd pulled his arms around her. He realised that they hadn't eaten at all the previous day. He'd make sure they both had breakfast before they went to work. He'd make porridge or pancakes, whatever she fancied.

Saturday had been a good day. They'd stayed in bed until late and gone to Asda. They'd even had a laugh pretending they were spies or detectives. Emma wore her oversized khaki jacket and kept speaking into her sleeve. They'd hid round corners and peered at that weird guy on the cheese counter. Even the security guard had noticed their strange behaviour. He'd followed them around for a bit. He was that lad he knew from school. The quiet one, in the year below. What was his name? He couldn't remember.

Saturday was a good day. Yesterday he wanted to forget. He pulled his, now numb, arm from under Emma's head and went downstairs to make breakfast.

CHAPTER 36

Robert

Robert rode his motorbike to work. He enjoyed the freedom of it. It surprised him that he was actually getting pleasure from overtaking queues of traffic. From not having to sit next to ripe smelling strangers on the bus. He arrived early and shackled his Bandit to the railings next to the office.

Mariam was making tea for Jack. She smiled when he entered the office. 'Do you want a cup,' she said.

'He hasn't got time,' said Jack. 'We've got a load of work on. It must be Spring; the roof companies want scaffolding set up all over the city and that job at the new estate is ready. I'll need a load of stuff putting up there. The other lads aren't here yet, but you can start checking the jobs off for me.'

Mariam raised her eyebrows at Robert, who smiled at her. 'It's going to be one of those days,' she said.

A few hours later, Robert was finishing off a job when he felt his phone vibrate in his back pocket. He wasn't allowed to take his phone out on the scaffold, it was one of Jack's rules. 'Sackable offence, mate'. He knew it was mainly because one of the crew liked to gamble. If he had his phone out he'd be putting a bet on or playing the slots, slacking in other words, but everyone had to suffer.

Robert managed to get down the ladder just in time to catch the call. It was Simon Porter.

He was straight to the point, 'Jane wants you and Emma to come for a meal on Friday after 6pm. Can you make it?'

'Yes,' said Robert.

'Fine, we will see you then.' Robert started to reply but realised that Simon had already put the phone down. He stared at it wondering what on earth Simon wanted.

CHAPTER 37

Emma

Emma walked to work most days. Today she felt uncomfortable. The stares she learned to cope with months ago. At first, she wanted to carry a billboard sign with "Yes, I'm the mother" printed on it. No one ever came right out and asked her. Stopped her and said, 'Are you that poor child's parent?'

She overheard two women once as she walked down the high street. They were huddled together, co-conspirators whispering. *I heard they were out clubbing and left that baby alone…no wonder she got out and went to the park…they deserved it then…hope they never have another.* Emma considered confronting them. Turning them around so they faced her. Demanding that they tell her to her face what they had said. But she didn't. She just walked to work with tears streaming down her face. Then locked herself in the staff toilets until she stopped crying. Her face was so red and blotchy, she was assigned to the back room.

Memories don't fade, their effect just gets weaker. Emma pulled her PVC jacket tightly around her and kept walking. Still sensing the stares and the pitiful glares. The rhythm of her steady pace calmed her.

Passing the newsagent, the small wooden sign out front was missing its white paper headline. The owner Mr. Kandesi knew Emma walked this way, she guessed the sign read *No Clues in Blonde Girl Murder* or *Parent's Misery at Losing Samantha*. Emma never read the papers. They lied. One day she would thank Mr. Kandesi for his kindness.

There was a queue outside the bookshop. Emma nearly turned and ran, she couldn't face a hoard. Maybe, they were reporters. But they didn't look the type. They had kind faces. Maybe, it was a coincidence. The shop was a little late opening. Emma headed for the back door, avoiding the scrum. Her boss opened it. He'd seen her coming. 'Front or back?' he asked.

Could she face them? 'Front.' She walked in and hung up her coat. Putting on her brave mask, she entered the front of the shop.

CHAPTER 38

Emma

Emma worked on the till. By the afternoon, it was unusually quiet. She couldn't help watching the customers in the shop. Some were walking slowly along the aisles peering at the titles, rarely touching or taking out a book. Some stood with a puzzled look on their face, perhaps trying to think of the name of that author they liked. Some flittered from genre to genre, while some always stayed in one section of the shop. The crime lovers were worse for this, Emma had noticed. They rarely strayed from their dedicated shelves. Often staying with the same authors until they'd devoured all of their titles. She wouldn't see them for a couple of weeks then they'd return and do the same to another author's works, like a swarm of flies.

She'd had seen some funny requests for books over the last few months. There was even that guy with the weird centre parting who wanted to order a book about costume design and wig making. He looked like he'd been spending too long in the gym. Over developed. Top heavy. It seemed such a strange request. Maybe he'd bought it for someone else.

Or that young girl, who wanted Zen and the Art of Motorcycle Maintenance. She'd only looked about 12. She had been carrying a pink rucksack with a notebook sticking out of the top.

Her daydreaming came to an abrupt halt. The woman in front of her was jabbing a copy of a Patricia Cornwell at her to get her attention. 'Did you not get enough sleep last night? Out clubbing were you?' the woman in a two piece suit snapped.

'Sorry,' said Emma and took the book. 'That will be £6.99.'

The woman huffed at her and left the shop, leaving Emma to her daydreaming again. Thinking if she got the chance later, she'd tell Charly all about that horrible, rude woman.

CHAPTER 39

w

The wig maker went downstairs to fetch some more hair out of the bag he kept hidden at the back of the sink. He'd fixed a new board just behind the waste pipe. A hard push and it would open on a spring. He put his hand into the flat canvas bag, with a picture of a paperback on it. He grabbed a large handful of blonde hair, realising as he did so that there wasn't much left.

He would need to go hunting again. Need to enter the killing field. He planned out his next move in that corner of his mind with the half open door. Where his secrets were kept just like the hidey hole under the sink. The place where he could touch and smell the long blonde hair of virginal angels. The place no one could see when they glimpsed the average guy with the regular job. The place where darkness lurked, stalked and killed.

CHAPTER 40

Emma

Emma lay on the settee covered by a grey, fleecy throw. She'd just watched the news. There was no mention of Charly or even Sam. This disappointed her. She'd wanted to hear something. Anything. Were they looking for a particular witness or car? Had they found any evidence from the scene? Were they hopeful of an arrest? Anything was better than nothing.

A few minutes later, Emma heard the roar of Robert's Bandit as it entered their street. She got up, went into the kitchen and switched on the kettle. Calmly putting Yorkshire tea bags into two mugs and adding the milk.

Robert entered the kitchen. 'Simon called me today,' he said.

Emma smiled and added the water to the two mugs. 'What did he want? Does Jane need my help?'

'He wants us to come to dinner on Friday after 6.' He swirled the teabag around in his mug. He never took it out until it was stewed a deep brown.

'Really. That's brilliant! But I've got nothing to wear.' She looked down at her old black trousers and white blouse that she wore for work. The rest of the time she wore black jeans or leggings with various band tee shirts and hoodies. She only had one pair of shoes and a couple of pairs of Doc Marten boots.

Robert smiled. 'You'll think of something.'

'What could they want? Do you think they've heard something about their daughter's death?'

'I've no idea. He didn't say.' Robert looked concerned.

His brow furrowed.

Emma took the teabag out of her tea. 'You look tired. Did you have a rough day?'

'I'm fine, it was busy, but you know me I like to work.'

Emma added, 'It stops me thinking', in her head. She took a sip of scolding tea. It burnt her lip. She blew on it before taking another sip. The roof of her mouth began to furrow. She ran her tongue along it. Feeling the ridges and just a little discomfort.

CHAPTER 41

Emma

Emma was sat up in bed flicking through Facebook posts on her her iPad. Robert was asleep beside her. He was gently snoring. She contemplated getting up and sitting on the settee. Moving downstairs, having the hum of a film on in the background, so she wouldn't disturb him. But then decided she liked looking down at him as he slept. Looking at the gentle curl to his blond eyelashes and the loose wispy new hairs at his temple. The ones not ready to wind around his dreads.

Martina was on line. Her son, Jay, had been killed in a fight in a pub seven years ago. One unlucky punch. She was one of the night owls. She'd nap during the day when she could and would be awake most of the night. She'd recently got a job as a Chat Monitor on a bingo site and seemed to be doing much better. Emma had asked her what she should wear to a meal at a house, somewhere posh, like Drapers. Her response lit up the screen:

Marty23: *How on earth should I know. The only time I've been near anywhere like Drapers is when I've been cleaning people's houses.*

Charlysmum: *Should I get something formal or casual?*

Marty23: *It's only been a few weeks. You could turn up in a bin bag and they wouldn't notice. What do you think they want anyway!? It's all a bit weird if you ask me!*

Charlysmum: *I don't know. Simon didn't say.*

Marty23: *It's not like you've got much in common though is it. What on earth will you talk about?*

Charlysmum: *Our kid's murders maybe.*

Emma was getting frustrated with Martina. She was fine if you wanted to talk about feelings and how much pain you are in. She knew all about the different stages of grief. But try and talk to her about anything remotely practical and she hadn't got a clue.

There were others that knew all about the law or how to set up a charity or a trust for your child. They had made it their mission to find something positive out of all of the grief and horror. They would know what to wear. They often had to speak at functions and attend formal dinners. They weren't online much though as they were too busy.

Emma sometimes wished she could be like them. She wished she could put her feelings into words so that people would listen. She couldn't even do the original television appeal. Robert's dad had done it in the end.

The Group wasn't just UK based, either, so often any advice or help was culturally based. One message was always clear though. Women, particularly mothers, cope or don't cope in different ways. There were no hard and fast rules. Just good days and bad days. Days you could cope and days you couldn't. Days you could put on a brave face and days you couldn't get out of bed. Days when you wanted to scream. Days when you could smile at a random happy thought.

Emma thought of the day that Charly was a bridesmaid for her cousin's wedding and remembered that she did have a strappy, flowery dress. Charly had asked her to buy it, so she wasn't the only one looking like "a girly girl". It was in the suitcase on top of the wardrobe. That would do, as she couldn't face shopping. She could lend her mum's high heels to go with it.

CHAPTER 42

Nicole

The bite-marked blocks came tumbling down and Rosie giggled so much she began to hiccup. She waved her arms around as if to say — again, again!

Nicole started to rebuild the bricks. One on top of each other. A red one followed by a blue one. She pulled her dressing gown tighter round her. She'd forgotten to add the fabric belt again after she'd washed it and was worried it might gape open. There was only Rosie and her at home though. Holly was staying at her dads. She wouldn't be dropped home for hours.

As Rosie knocked down the bricks again, Nicole sighed. She pushed her overlong mousy hair behind her ears. She'd tried tying it up in a ponytail, but Rosie always grabbed at the hairbands with her chunky little hands and pulled them out. She was attempting to grow it, but knew it was no good. She was going to have to get it cut. It may not be the current style to have short, spiky hair but needs must.

She looked over at the open books on the table. Her assignment was due tomorrow and it still needed referencing. She hoped she would have time to finish it later. She couldn't ask for another extension. Her tutor had made that clear.

The washing machine had stopped. It was making that noise again. Beep, beep, beep. She wished she hadn't taken it off her sister's hands. The incessant noise drove her nuts. She picked up Rosie and a handful of the bricks, placing them in the middle of the playpen.

She had to hang the washing out in the yard. The hair began to prickle on the back of her neck as she pulled the damp washing from the machine. It was mostly the kids. Pretty little dresses, odd socks and misshapen cardigans. It would take her ages to hang them on the rotary dryer.

She hated going into the yard. She always felt like someone was watching her. It was overlooked by a number of other terraced houses and she daren't look up at any of the windows in case she spotted someone staring back down at her. It didn't seem to matter that she knew most of her neighbours. She'd been feeling this way for days. The fabric belt was on top of the machine, so she quickly tied it round her waist. She shivered, as she put on her slipper boots and stepped outside.

CHAPTER 43

W

The wig maker couldn't use the tree anymore to spy on his victims. It had become a shrine where people came to mourn or simply stare grotesquely at the "place where those murders of little girls happened".

Instead he now stood in the stairwell of a block of flats facing the Longmere Estate. He could see the woman in the yard hanging out the washing. She kept brushing her hair behind her ears with her hand. The clothes she hung were all her children's. But he had no interest in kids' clothes. He had no interest in children. Tapping a rhythm on the side of the binoculars, he watched as the woman in the dressing gown and slipper boots continued to hang out the washing.

There was no sign of her daughter with the long golden locks. The one who practised handstands against the yard wall. He would give it another ten minutes and try again tomorrow.

CHAPTER 44

DI Chambers

It was late on Thursday evening. A few of the officers on the Murder Investigation Team were still at their desks. A couple were crouched round a laptop reviewing more CCTV footage from the road leading to the forest's car park. So far they had traced a number of vehicles in the vicinity of the forest on the night of both Charlotte's and Samantha's murders. All of those traced had valid reasons for passing the forest at that time. They had not found the same vehicle on both nights, but they still had a small number to trace. Unfortunately, there wasn't any CCTV in the car park. The council could not afford to run and maintain it. They had to rely on the footage obtained from local businesses. The latest of which they had only recovered that afternoon. They had decided to widen the search to try and get a clearer picture of a couple of, so far, untraceable vehicles or drivers. Some because the number plate had been partially obscured, for example, by a passing jogger and one because the owner of the vehicle, Mike Deyton, denied using it on that night. Mike had a good alibi too, as he worked nights as a DJ and had taken his van to a local hotel, leaving his car on the drive.

DI Chambers prepared for Monday morning's staff briefing. He opened a new page of his legal pad.
He wrote:
Who?
    Charlotte Dean aged 6
    Samantha Porter aged 6

Living in opposite ends of the city
Did not attend the same school or any of the same clubs
Both had long blonde hair
Perpetrator: Unknown

When?
Charlotte Dean: Friday 11th November 2015, abducted approximately 6pm. Time of death between 6pm and 9:00pm
Samantha Porter: Friday 13th May 2016, abducted approximately 6:30pm. Time of death between 6:30pm and 10:00pm

Where?
Primary murder scene: Unknown
Moved to disposal site within five hours
Disposal site: edge of forest, next to car park on Sutton Road

What?
Murder weapon — kitchen knife, long blade with serrated edge
Both girls stabbed once in heart likely to have caused immediate death
Hair removed — shaved with a razor. Evidence of small cuts on both girl's head caused by scissor blades. Cut first and then shaved?

Why?
Why did he cut their hair? Unanswerable at this time
Why did he kill them? Unanswerable at this time

How?

Both bodies disposed at same site
No evidence killed in the vicinity of disposal site
Most likely brought to wood in a vehicle from unknown other location
Prior to this: in the weeks preceding abduction possibly stalked both victims
Sites where both children could have been seen (Charlotte's school and Samantha's back garden) are in direct sight from upper branches of tree that girls were dumped at
Victims and their mothers were regular visitors to the Asda Supermarket on Dane Road (Charlotte every Thursdays at 4:00pm approx.) (Samantha Tuesdays at 5pm approx.)

He was extremely concerned about Mike Deyton's car. He felt it was a key part of the enquiry. The Crime Scene Manager, Janet Taylor, had not yet agreed that they should treat the car as a crime scene. He thought this was a mistake and had called her a number of times to explain why. If evidence was lost because of this, it could prejudice the case. He wrote next steps: door to door in adjacent houses to Mike Deyton's address and removal of his car. He underlined the second point three times. He would have to convince Janet on Monday in front of both their colleagues.

A few minutes later, he closed his pad, tidied his desk, turned off the office lights and left. His thoughts immediately turning to home. There was a stew he'd prepared earlier in the slow cooker. His wife would have already eaten. They had a rule: if he was working after 6pm then he would text her. She wouldn't wait then for them to eat together. He would warm up something when he got home instead. It prevented all those "your dinner is in the dog" conversations. James got into his car, the thought of tucking into stew and crusty bread warmed him

CHAPTER 45

Emma

It was after 6pm on a Friday.

Emma and Robert had spent an hour discussing what to take to the Porters. They'd decided on wine, chocolates and a mixed bag of Haribos for the boys. Neither of them were big wine drinkers. Emma liked bottles of Newcastle Brown and Robert liked real ales, or lager if he had been working to quench his thirst. They decided to buy the red on offer at their local off license — a Chilean Merlot with plenty of spice, £8.99 reduced to £6.99 on special offer. Emma chose it because she liked the label. It was red with large diagonal writing.

Robert had hammered on the Porter's door. Emma scowled at him. Sometimes he didn't seem to know his own strength or what was appropriate.

Simon Porter opened the door. He looked pale and drawn. Emma noticed the flecks of grey at his temples, as he brushed his hair from his face before shaking her hand.

'Pleased to meet you,' he said politely.

Emma smiled at him and gave him a hug. He seemed unsure how to react keeping his arms by his side, but then held onto her bare shoulders for a few moments. Seemingly, glad of the contact.

A few moments later, Jane came to the door. Her eyes were red. She had clearly been crying. She rubbed her eyes, then wiped her hands on her navy blue apron.

'The boys are at their grandmother's,' she said quietly, as though that explained her tearful appearance.

Emma hugged her too. 'I understand,' she whispered.

Robert looked unsure what to do. Emma took his hand and led him into the house. He gave the plastic bag of offerings to Simon.

The meal they ate — homemade quiche and salad followed by strawberries and cream, Simon having forgotten to ask if they were vegetarian, was finished quickly. Neither of the sets of parents brought together in this random, horrific manner were able to start the conversation. The reason for them being together in the first place.

The men could talk about football. Emma was sure that after a minute, Simon had far surpassed Robert's knowledge on the subject as he preferred watching MotoGP and British Superbikes. This was confirmed when Robert started nodding instead of commenting on the state of Stanton Rovers.

Emma was relieved when the meal was over, and she could offer to help Jane in the kitchen with the washing up.

'Thank you, for inviting us,' she said to Jane, as she rinsed the dishes in the sink. The Porters had an industrial sized dishwasher, Emma felt slightly envious then realised there was nothing in either of their situations for anyone to be envious of.

'How do you ever cope?' Jane said. She was crying again.

'I guess everyone is different. I wear a mask. The "outside" Emma. The one that people see at work or at the shops or here tonight. Inside I'm in a million tiny pieces. Pieces that will never be put back together. They are just covered occasionally by the mask. A blanket...I'm sorry that's the best way I can describe it. Although there are good days mixed in with the bad. More now than before. Odd, random days when you notice the colours of the flowers or the softness of a piece of fabric. When there is a sliver of light in the world full of grey.'

'I've got to wear that mask for the boys, but I can't do it. I just disappear upstairs. I can't even play with them! What sort of mother am I!' Jane balled up the corners of her apron. Her eyes pleading with Emma. *Help me please.*

Emma sat Jane down at the kitchen table and poured her another large glass of the Merlot.

'Here,' she said and sat down next to her. 'You're still a mother. Not just a mother to your two boys but you're still Samantha's mother. No one can take that away.'

Jane didn't move. Didn't touch the wine. Didn't speak.

Emma continued, 'For the first few months nothing made any sense. There was no reality. Everything happened a million miles away. No one knew what to do or to say. No one knew how to connect to me. My world became a silent place. Even Robert wasn't a part of it. He just went to work, came home and occasionally tried to force feed me.' Emma smiled. 'I think he thought he was about to lose me. That I'd starve to death.'

Jane still stared blankly, concentrating on some imaginary spot.

Emma drank some of more wine. Its acidity burned down her throat. She welcomed it. 'It does get better. You think it never will, but it does.'

She touched Jane's arm. Jane looked at her then and smiled the briefest smile. 'I'm not Samantha's mother. My daughter is dead.'

Then Jane stood up and started to scrub the worktops.

CHAPTER 46

Robert

Simon was clearly wrestling with something. He kept offering Robert another lager despite his full glass. Neither of them spoke. Robert kept glancing towards the kitchen door, hoping Emma would come in and save him.

Finally, Simon spoke, 'I wanted to ask you whether you saw Charly after...'

After. After what? Then it clicked. Simon meant after she was killed.

'No. I couldn't. My dad did the identification. I couldn't face it. Emma couldn't either. We decided that we wanted to remember her before not after,' Robert said slowly.

'I haven't told Jane. I don't want her to know. Sam had her head covered and the rest of her body. I could only see her face through the glass. I thought it was odd. I couldn't see her hair. Just her face. There wasn't a mark on it. Not a scratch. Was it the same for...for Charly?'

'I don't know,' Robert admitted. He had never asked his dad what Charly had looked like lying there. In fact, he rarely spoke to his dad at all. He'd not been able to find the right words. It was as though his seeing Charly after had created this chasm between them. He knew he was going to have to go and see his dad. Find out if the same was true for Charly. Travel the fifty miles there as soon as possible.

'I need to find out, don't I. I'll ring you, when I've spoken to my dad,' Robert said.

Silence fell again. There was nothing left to say, so

Robert went to call Emma. It was time to leave.

CHAPTER 47

Emma

Emma followed behind Robert who seemed in a rush to get away from Drapers. His attention seemed focused at some point straight ahead and he was doing his darnedest not to have to stop and talk to Emma about the evening.

Eventually, Emma just stopped walking. Her feet were killing her in her mum's shoes. She never wore heels and the shoes were a size too small. Robert didn't stop. 'Rob…!' Emma attempted to call him and then gave up. Whatever was in his head was clearly more important than she was at the moment.

The kerb looked inviting, but that was probably the effect of the wine. Emma sat down between a Ford Escort and a Kia. After taking her shoes off, she placed her elbows on her thighs, held her chin in her hands and sighed. It was about a mile walk to get home and they'd spent all their spare cash on the treats for the Porters. She couldn't even get a taxi.

As she considered her options, she felt a hand on her shoulder. She jumped and twisted round to see Robert on his knees behind her. 'Where did you go? Took me a minute to realise you weren't behind me.'

'My feet were killing, and you seemed to want to jog home.' Emma turned her back on him and faced the road again.

Robert started to massage her shoulders. Emma smiled and said, 'It's my feet that are killing.'

He shuffled next to her on the kerb and sat with his legs stretched out in front of him. 'Stick them up here then,' he said, gesturing to his legs.

Emma complied, only to topple backwards against the bumper of the Kia. They both held their breath, expecting the alarm to go off. It didn't. They burst out laughing. Robert began to massage her feet, squeezing her toes tightly between his thumb and fingers. 'Ummm, that's better,' Emma laughed.

'Glad to be of service, madam.'

Emma leant over and kissed him. He tasted of lager and strawberries. She didn't mind.

She broke away and said, 'What did the Porters want? Did you find out?'

Robert looked up the street, 'No, Simon didn't say. Maybe he thought you could help his wife?'

Emma sighed. 'She just cried, and I passed her the wine. What can you say?'

A tabby cat scuttled by, turned to glance at them and darted off.

Robert finished massaging Emma's feet and squeezed her thigh. 'I want to take you home.' He moved her feet back into the road and stood.

Emma stood and started to put her mum's shoes back on, wincing as she did so. She lost her balance and leaned on the Kia's bonnet. The car alarm pierced the still night air and the cat bolted past her. Emma put her hand to her mouth and started to giggle. Robert pulled on her arm. 'Come on. Let's get you home before they call the police on us.'

CHAPTER 48

Robert

For the rest of the walk home, Robert thought about two things. The first and perhaps most pressing being how much he wanted to get home and kiss Emma again. But the other thought that kept crashing in was, why had he lied to her? Why couldn't he tell his wife that Samantha's head was covered? They'd never been told that Charly was damaged in any way. They knew that Charly had been stabbed, just once and that had killed her. But they hadn't been told anything else.

Robert remembered asking that question. The one all father's had to ask, 'had the bastard abused his daughter?' The reply had been immediate and reassuring. 'No, there was absolutely no evidence of that.' It still gnawed at him though. Turned his insides into writhing mush. That fear that some madman had got off on butchering his daughter. Had been sexually aroused by it. He forgot about Emma then. The urgency to get home dissipated.

Until she squeezed his hand. He realised she was limping. Leaning in to her, he whispered into her ear, 'It's not far now.'

He noticed her shiver. They hadn't bought jackets with them. It had been warm earlier. So, he put his arm around her shoulders and pulled her to him. She looked up at him with the laughing eyes of someone who was ever so slightly tipsy. He pecked her on the lips, but she was having none of that. She kissed him back hard. The urge to rush home returned in an instant. He picked her up and carried her, loved the feel of her arms around his neck, holding on tight like his baby girl.

CHAPTER 49

Emma

Emma woke the next morning with a pounding head. She didn't think that she'd drunk that much at the Porters. They hadn't got to sleep until at least half past three, Emma smiled as she remembered the previous night's events. Robert had reminded her how much she fancied him. He could be a considerate lover when he chose to be. But she'd rarely given him the chance over the last six months. She'd missed the closeness, the letting go.

Robert must have known that she was awake. He opened his eyes and stared at her placing his arm across her belly and hugging her close. 'I hope you weren't thinking of leaving me,' he said.

'I was only going as far as the bathroom.' Emma laughed. The good thing about dreads is that they looked the same whatever the time of the day. Emma's spiky hair stood out at all angles until she attacked it with gel. For some reason she had decided that she wanted to look her best for Robert but now it was too late. He leant towards her and kissed her. She was aware that she hadn't brushed her teeth yet. He didn't seem to care.

'You can go now,' he said.

She threw her pillow at him as she got out of bed. He tapped it away and it landed on the floor next to his side. Emma guessed that she'd have trouble getting it back off him on her return.

The post clattered through the letterbox as she crossed the landing. Emma wasn't sure whether to bother going to fetch it. It was usually bills or adverts for stuff they didn't want or couldn't afford. She decided bathroom first, then she'd go and check on the post.

By the time Emma had finished in the bathroom, Robert had already got up and fetched the post. He was in the kitchen reading a letter. His face was etched with the tightness of anger. A plain brown envelope was open on the worktop. The address handwritten. It was addressed to her. Emma Dean not Robert. Why had he opened her letter? She attempted to take the letter from him, but he just grasped it tighter and pulled it towards his chest.

'It's addressed to me, Robert. Give it to me.'

'Believe me, Em. You don't want to see it.' He wasn't looking at her, why? Was he embarrassed by what he'd done? Ashamed?

'You can't open my mail...You just can't. How dare you!' Emma screeched.

'I've had them, Em. Too many to mention. All from the same person,' he sighed. 'You don't want to read it. Trust me.'

'I can be my own judge. You can't make that decision for me. Please, give it to me.'

He held the letter out to her then. Emma took it. Her hands shook as she began to read. There was no introduction. No address. No Dear Emma. The letter began: *You should have aborted your foetus. You didn't deserve a daughter, you green haired freak. I bet you've spent more on tattoos and piercings than you have toys. I bet Charly was a mistake that got in the way of your drug taking and partying.* Emma stopped reading. 'How many of these have we had?'

'A few. I'm sorry, Em. I didn't want to worry you.'

'Worry me?...Have you told the police? Patrice...Have you told Patrice?'

'What's the point, do you think they'll be interested in this shit?' Robert grabbed the letter then and started to crumple it in his fist.

'Stop! Let me finish reading it.'

Robert stopped crumpling it but didn't let it go. Emma's heart pounded. She wanted to grab her husband's hand and tear the letter from his fist, but she knew it would be pointless. He handled planks for a living and she handled books. Two very different parts of the same tree. She was far stronger than Robert in many ways and certainly not the weaker sex but in terms of brute force he would win. She had to be subtler.

'I need to finish reading it or what I'll imagine it saying could be far worse.' Emma held her hand out. Robert gave her the letter. She lay it on the worktop and attempted to flatten it out. *You and your dreadlocked husband are freaks. I hope you never have more children.*

Never have more children. Why was this stranger, this vile accuser allowed to mention more children when she couldn't? She couldn't speak of more children in case anyone thought she was replacing her daughter. The letter writer or the wider world had no clue how hard it had been to have Charly. The first year they tried for a baby, nothing happened. The doctors they saw were quick to say that there was no medical reason that she couldn't conceive. Maybe they were trying too hard? Then she'd resorted to ovulation strips. Texting Robert the moment that she found she was the most fertile. It didn't matter if he was up a ladder on the other side of Stanton, she expected him to rush home as quickly as possible. Sex became clinical. Until she caught. Only to then have a miscarriage. Emma was ready to give up when she caught for Charly. But the writer wouldn't know this and wouldn't care how much their words cut deep into her soul.

'They think we're freaks, Em.'

Emma tore the letter into tiny pieces and threw it into the kitchen bin. Instantly regretting it. What if it was from the killer? But chances were it was some bored housewife with nothing better to do than inflict pain on others,

Neither of them were freaks. They were just different. Emma hugged her husband, buried her face in his 'locks. 'So, what do you want to do? Cut your dreads off? Buy a suit? Get a job in an office? We can't be led by these idiots.'

Robert hugged Emma to him. Held her closer. It reminded her of the night before not the letter. He whispered, 'Maybe you could grow your hair long and pin it back into a messy bun?' Her shoulders went first. The giggle took hold, until it could no longer be shackled. Emma laughed out loud and stroked Robert's dreads. 'Don't you ever cut these off. Even when you're ninety, do you hear.'

What she didn't do was talk about having another baby. She couldn't talk about that. She could stop taking the pill. Leave it to fate, but she'd done that weeks ago.

CHAPTER 50

Nicole

Nicole had run out of nappies. It was nearly Holly's bedtime, but she had to go out and get some or Rosie wouldn't have a fresh nappy for the morning. She'd worked solidly on her essay all morning and had sent it into the academic ether before the cutoff time. She'd then spent a couple of hours cleaning, before lying down on the settee for an hour dozing with Rosie. By the time she picked Holly up from school, despite walking straight past the shops, she'd forgotten that she needed nappies, milk and bread.

There was only one thing for it. Holly and Rosie would have to forgo a bath tonight and she would have to pop into Asda. She'd even get herself a pizza and a frozen Banoffee Pie. She'd worked hard. She deserved it.

Twenty minutes later and Nicole was pushing Rosie round the aisles in the shopping cart. As ever, she'd chosen one with a dodgy wheel. Holly had to keep helping her push the stubborn trolley in the right direction. A couple of times they'd still managed to hit the metal at the bottom of the displays. The shopping trolley had lurched, and Rosie had giggled. Nothing ever seemed to faze her.

Just as Nicole approached the frozen section, she started feeling apprehensive again. She wasn't sure why she felt so uneasy. She usually didn't mind looking after the kids alone. Yes, it was tiring. Yes, she got lonely for adult company. And yes, it got in the way of her studies. But she loved not having to seek agreement for every trip to the shops or to discuss what she was having for tea each night. She was proud that she'd got through two years of her English Literature degree. Only taking a year out in the middle to have Rosie. Both her children's dads were nigh on useless anyway. Neither wanted the full time responsibility of fatherhood.

But unusually she wished she wasn't alone tonight. She quickly went to the checkout, paid for what she had managed to collect, not bothering with the Banoffee Pie and left. She almost ran across the car park pushing Rosie in her buggy. Holly barely keeping up holding on to the buggy's frame as tight as she could. Nicole only felt safe when she'd reached home and slammed the front door.

CHAPTER 51

W

    The wig maker couldn't believe his luck. The girl with the long blonde locks had been bought to him. At one point he was close enough to the virgin undyed, unbleached hair that he could almost smell it. Her mother was so desperate to get all her items through the checkout that she hadn't noticed him standing next to her daughter. If he'd had the chance, he would have followed them home, but he was working, and it would be noticed if he simply took her in the street. 'Patience is a virtue', his mother would have said.

    His sister, on the other hand, would have said, "Grab life with both hands and to hell with the consequences!" He took after his mother. His sister was too flighty and easily led. It would be her downfall.

    He'd learned what happened when you tried to take them in the street. They fought back.

CHAPTER 52

Emma

The sun blazed on Saturday morning. Nothing but a blue sky as far as you could see. The occasional cloud drifted softly, casting a fleeting shadow across the garden. Emma called it a garden, but it was more of a backyard. There was just enough room for the green plastic table and two chairs that sat by the kitchen window. Robert had planted seeds in tubs and these had managed to grow over the last few months. Despite the neglect, the first of the violas with their brassy colours had started to bloom.

Emma was drinking a coffee, alone, at the table. She looked up and saw a flock of racing pigeons begin their regular swoop above their house. She wasn't sure who trained them, but at least three times a day they were let out and would sweep above the terraced houses in their street. You would sometimes see a number of them together or sometimes they would settle into a formation of twos and threes. Emma always enjoyed watching them. During that time, she didn't think of anything else.

Robert had left on his bike early. He said that he was going to see a friend in Crowborough. He said it was someone he used to work with and he'd asked if he could help him with a foreigner. A foreigner just meant a job on the side — cash in hand. Not that they needed the money now, they hardly ever went anywhere, and Emma couldn't remember the last time she'd treated herself.

She had to work in the shop for a few hours that afternoon to cover for someone who was going to a friend's wedding. Maybe she'd go into town early and buy some new clothes. She could stop off on the way back at Asda and buy something special for tea. It would be a surprise for Robert when he got back from work.

She sat there for a little while longer. Until she heard the slam of a back door three doors down. It was quickly followed by the giggly laughter of two young sisters. Emma sighed. Debating whether to go inside. Then over the fence floated three large, perfect bubbles filled with tiny rainbows. She watched them burst — one, two, three.

Emma drained her coffee and went back inside to get changed for work.

CHAPTER 53

Robert

The journey had been uneventful. The bike swooped and soared effortlessly through both country lanes and small towns. Gear changes glided into place. Speed rose and fell. Corners hovered on the skyline and were taken with precision and faultless timing, the bike flicking from side to side.

Despite the constant hum and roar of the engine, the journey gave Robert the chance to contemplate the meeting ahead. He knew any conversation with his dad was going to be difficult. He hadn't spoken to him in so long. They had lost the ability to communicate. Robert tried to remember the conversations they'd had before Charly's death. What had these two grown men spoken about? He recalled that they usually talked about bands and bikes. His dad had been a bass player in a seventies rock band. One of those brilliant in your local pub — but never quite making it bands. They both shared a love of music with a number of bands they both followed and had seen on numerous occasions. For the first few years of gig going, Robert had sat on his dad's shoulders watching in muddy fields; the last few gigs, they had shared the mosh pit together, dripping in sweat and singing loudly.

Then Robert thought of the bikes. The old Honda CB500 that had stood gleaming in their garage until Robert's mum had insisted his dad sell it as she feared *it was encouraging Robert to ride*. It was too late by then Robert had regularly ridden his mate's scrambler in the fields behind their house, although he could barely touch the ground. He remembered the day his dad handed over the keys to the CB to the greying, spindly dealer who wanted to 'add it to his collection'. He'd felt sorry for his dad and his end of an era downhearted look.

It was odd though, Robert could still speak to his mum about everything. She often phoned in the evening when his dad had gone to the pub. They would talk about their day in detail. His mum had recently admitted that she wanted to go and live in Australia with his brother Adam. She wanted to be near her other grandchildren. She didn't say surviving grandchildren, but she may well have done. Robert could understand why they were leaving but it had really upset him. He hadn't told Emma yet. He wasn't sure why. He was always so careful what he told Emma. She was still so fragile. He'd decided, though, that today after talking with his dad that he would tell his mum that they should go with his blessing.

Half an hour later, he pulled up outside their house. It was a small cottage in the heart of a village. They had downsized and sold everything to get it three years ago. They wanted to grow their own veg and be close to a friendly country pub. They had, so far, only managed to make use of the pub; or at least his dad had. They were working on the growing their own. They'd managed a few tomatoes and carrots this year. It clearly hadn't been as idyllic as they'd hoped though if they were planning to up sticks and move to Australia.

His mum kissed him on the cheek and made herself scarce when he arrived as he'd pre-warned her that he wanted to speak to his dad on his own. She had made a pot of tea as soon as he pulled up and had placed it on the dining room table with two large slices of cake. His dad sat down and started pouring a cup for himself and Robert.

'Your mum said that you had something to ask me,' he said, not wasting any time with pleasantries.

'It's about Charly,' Robert began.

'Yes. I'd guessed as much,' his dad said. 'It must have bought it all back there being another one. Your mum has been in tears about it. She won't tell you that though. She's trying to be your rock. It's been very hard for her.'

'I'm sorry. I never expected her to be.'

'Why are you apologising, she's your mother. It's what they do.'

'I've never said this, but I'm really grateful that you took control when Charly died. I couldn't do it. I couldn't have seen her. Lying there. Like that.'

'I'm not going to pretend it was easy, but it had to be done. I don't blame you for not doing it. It doesn't make you less of a father.'

Less of a father. What a thing to say. Robert had always thought his grief made him a loving father. The fact that he hadn't been able to protect his beautiful, little girl made him less of a father. Everything after her death had been irrelevant. Up until now.

'We had a meal with the Porters yesterday. It was something Simon said...I've got to check it out...He said that his daughter, Sam, had her head covered when he saw her...after.'

'It's funny you should say that. I thought it was odd at the time. Yes...yes Charly was the same. She was wearing a white headscarf pulled tight round her head. All you could see was her beautiful face. I recognised it, of course, straight away. I will never forget how she looked...She looked like the perfect angel in a school play. I always imagine her lying there with wings and instead of the scarf, a little halo. It helps me somehow.'

Robert had been holding his head, pulling at his locks as his dad spoke. He was wearing the pink hairband today. He hadn't for a few weeks, but he needed it today. He looked up when his dad had finished speaking and saw that his dad was crying. He'd never seen him crying before...ever. Even at Charly's funeral. Robert remembered how he had stood to one side ordering everyone about. Making sure everything was done just right.

'I've never spoken to anyone about this before,' his dad continued. 'I'm glad you've asked in a way. I wasn't sure what you wanted or needed to know...I feel dreadful that I didn't ask the police why they'd covered her head, but I just answered their questions...I wanted the whole ordeal to be over as quickly as possible.'

Robert got up out of his chair and hugged his dad. They both stood together for minutes. The gulf between them erased. He stayed for lunch then rode back home. On the way he remembered he'd said nothing about Australia. But now, he decided, he didn't want them to go so perhaps that was for the best.

CHAPTER 54

Emma

Emma arrived at work. As she was rushing to hang up her jacket in her locker, she felt a hand on her shoulder. She jumped. It was only her boss.

'Sorry I'm late,' Emma mumbled.

'No, that's fine.' Dave tapped her on the arm. 'Come to my office. Let's have a little chat.'

Emma would have preferred just to start work. Slipping behind the front desk. Speaking to strangers in a dancing, happy made-up voice. But she followed her boss. He paid her wages.

As soon as she sat down on one of the uncomfortable tiny chairs that he'd squeezed into the broom cupboard of an office, Dave started to speak, 'Emma you've worked here for four years. You're my most trusted employee. I know we've had to make allowances over the last six months.' He was blushing and staring at the floor.

Emma wondered if this was it. That he'd finally had enough of making allowances and was about to hand over her cards.

Emma rolled the bottom of her shirt in her hands, creasing it.

Dave continued, 'I'm worried about you Em. I used to catch you lifting up books and smelling them. Turning the pages, smiling at phrases that pleased you. Popping the books back on the shelf. Glancing round to check if anyone had seen you.' He sighed. 'You don't do that anymore. When was the last time you read, Em?'

This was unexpected. He wasn't sacking her. This was empathy. Not the odd ridiculous cliché of sympathy. She had to bite her lip to stop the tears. He was right, so absolutely right.

'I can't read. I open a book. Turn to a page. Look at the words. They mean nothing.' It was Emma's turn to stare at the ground.

Dave leant forward on his desk, clasping his hands together. 'What's your favourite book?'

Emma smiled. 'The Bone People, by Keri Hulme.'

'I'm assuming you've got a copy. If not, I can get you one.'

'Yes, I've got a copy at home.' It was on the bookshelf Robert had made for her. It had taken him weeks and it wobbled, not that she would ever tell him.

'Read it. Even if it's just one page a day. You probably know what lies on each page anyway, so gaps won't worry you. Just read it, Em.'

Who would have thought that the best advice would come from her boss. He was right, without books she was lost. She'd replaced the velvet richness of stories with words read on social media. The caresses of the sea eating the earth, with holiday snaps and 'wish you were heres'. The grief of a father trying to untangle the complex knots of a surviving relationship, with an angry mother ranting in profanities. She was awash with empty, vacant, unfeeling words.

CHAPTER 55

Nicole

  Nicole was awake early. Her two daughters were still sleeping. Rosie lay in the cot next to Nicole's bed and Holly was in the other bedroom. Nicole watched her baby daughter sleeping. She kept searching round for her dummy. Spitting it out and then unconsciously reaching for it with her hand and putting it back in. Sucking at it a couple of times then spitting it out again.
  Nicole thought of her university friends. They would be lying in bed asleep at this hour, dreaming about the night before. They'd been an indie band playing at SUSU. If she'd been a normal student, she'd have been drinking jagerbombs in the student union bar before dancing the night away. Instead, she'd watched the television until Rosie had fallen asleep in her lap. Then had an early night. Perhaps this was better than having a drunken night of all soon forgotten passion with the union president and regrets in the morning.
  Still there were no essays to write today, so she planned to take them both to the park. It was supposed to be hot. One of those scorching May days. Hotter than the summer was likely to be. She decided to make a picnic. They could pick up some crisps and sausage rolls from Asda on the way.
  She yawned and rolled over, hugging the pillow and attempted to snooze for a few more minutes. Thoughts drifting into her mind of lager tasting kisses and soft caresses, interrupted by the all too real sound of footsteps padding along the landing. The door to the bedroom opened and Holly climbed into bed next to her. They snuggled up for a Sunday morning

cuddle.

CHAPTER 56

W

The Wig Maker had no work today. He'd woken early and taken up his spot in the stairwell of the flats on the Longmere estate. It was a beautiful day. You could see for miles up here. The blue sky was uninterrupted, except for a flock of pigeons that were circling above the Chantries. Swooping and gliding in formation. Not diverging from their path. Round and round.

The girl with the golden locks wasn't in the yard. But the Wig Maker noticed the washing billowing on the rotary washing line. Her mum must have forgotten to get it in yesterday. He hoped that she'd come out soon and the girl would be with her. Either helping her with the washing or practicing her handstands. Maybe she would stay outside on her own. It would only take five minutes to drive from here to their house.

Tapping an uneven rhythm on the bannister with a button on his jacket, he continued to wait. Tap, tap, pause, tap, tap, tap, pause, tap, pause, tap, tap, tap.

He knew how to subdue, steal and spirit away. Girls were easy. They weighed less, didn't fight back or have the foresight to scream.

CHAPTER 57

Nicole

Nicole had just finished making sandwiches when she realised she hadn't bought in yesterday's washing. She picked up the green plastic washing basket and went into the yard. Leaving Holly and Rosie inside playing with the multi-coloured wooden bricks.

There was no uneasiness today. Nicole's thoughts were on swings, slides and eating sandwiches on a tartan picnic blanket. She remembered they'd run out of suncream and would need to get that too on the way.

As soon as the washing was brought in and the bag was packed full of food and squash, they all left the house.

Ten minutes later, they were scouting the aisles for other nice things to eat. Waiting at the checkout. Nicole overheard snatches of conversation. *Josh not working today...I stayed at Steve's last night. I haven't been home yet...good, he gives me the creeps...my mum will go mad when I get in. She thinks I should have dumped him.* She paid quickly. Excitedly, they all rushed to the park, wanting to get there before the crowds.

CHAPTER 58

DI Chambers

DI Chambers sat at the dining table surrounded by his family. Presents were piled high on the sideboard. His wife's attempt at baking his birthday cake was carefully positioned in the centre of the dining table. His parents had even come up from Devon. He was pleased that, for once, they'd had an unspoiled Sunday dinner. No calls, no interruptions.

His daughter, Rhian, had even stopped studying long enough to eat her meal at the table with them. She was preparing for her viva. Her doctoral thesis was on something to do with the high rates of dyslexia amongst the prison population. He could never remember the exact title. To be honest, he wasn't much concerned about the reasons for criminality. He just dealt with the realities of it. Rhian had tried, but failed, to debate him on the issue. *I always leave the conjecture to other people.* His usual response.

It was time to open the presents. He decided to open Rhian's first. She'd been so excited about it. He could tell. She was beaming as he carefully unwrapped it. Gently pulling the paper away from the sellotape and folding over the rough edges. She'd bought him a framed picture. There was the familiar profile of Sherlock Holmes in the corner, complete with deerstalker and the quote:

"*It is a capital mistake to theorise before one has data. Insensibly one begins to twist facts to suit theories instead of theories to suit facts.* Sherlock Holmes. A Scandal in Bohemia."

James laughed out loud. 'That's wonderful', he said and

hugged his daughter. 'I will put it up in my study as a reminder.'

'Not in your office?' Rhian said.

James had a photo of his wife and daughter in the office at the station. He changed it for a new one once a year. That was all he needed as a constant reminder of how lucky he was.

His mobile started to vibrate in his pocket. 'Excuse me,' he said, leaving his family and retiring to his study.

As he did so, his wife sighed and started to clear the table. His mum and dad raised their eyebrows and helped. Rhian went back to her studies.

The phone call concerned a breakthrough in the case. A member of the public had found a crumpled photograph of a teenager with blonde flowing locks in the bark of the tree. The tree where the girls were disposed. Sergeant Khapor thought DI Chambers would want to see it straight away. He did.

CHAPTER 59

W

The wig maker had returned home. Some of the local teenagers had spotted him in the stairwell and had given him the eye. They'd made sure that they'd shoulder barged him as they went past down the stairs. They hadn't come back or said anything. Maybe they'd been surprised at how hard he was. Solid muscle under the baggy t-shirt that he wore. He hadn't seen the girl. This frustrated him. He stared at the photograph he kept in his jeans pocket every day, one of many he had copied at Supersnaps all those years ago, and then at the wig. It was far from ready.

CHAPTER 60

DI Chambers

DI Chambers arrived at the station twenty minutes later. A copy of the photograph had been placed on display on the wall.

'We've sent it to be enhanced,' Sergeant Khapor said.

'Where exactly was it found?' asked DI Chambers.

'Alice Davies, Samantha's Primary School teacher, had gone up to the tree to lay some flowers this morning. She does this every Sunday apparently. There was a glint of the paper sticking out from part of the bark, which she forced out with her nails. She had some paper in her bag, so she wrapped it in that and brought it straight here.'

DI Chambers stared at the photograph. Despite being creased it was clearly of a teenager with blonde wavy hair. Not tight curls but perhaps lightly permed. He remembered seeing a lot of girls with hair just like that in the eighties and nineties. It was all the rage to have your hair crimped or what was it called...demi-waved?

Who was this woman? It was possible it was nothing to do with the case. Maybe it was a case of unrequited love or a break up that had led someone to force the photograph into the bark of the tree. It could have been their days, months, years. They'd scoured the tree after both murders, but things were often missed. He knew this was human nature. It was always a cause of annoyance.

There was a briefing set for Thursday. Despite this, DI Chambers decided that as soon as they had a reasonable enhancement in his hands, he was going to the press. He wanted it in every newspaper and on every news programme by the morning.

CHAPTER 61

Robert

Robert got up for work early on Monday morning. He didn't want to wake Emma, so he had the radio on low in the kitchen. He heard the announcer on the news say, 'Stanton police have issued a photograph of an individual they need to identify in relation to the Charlotte Dean and Samantha Porter case.'

Robert stopped buttering his toast, ran into the living room and switched on the television and shouted, 'Emma!'

They both stood rigid and stared at the television for what seemed like hours until the photograph came up on the screen.

'Oh my god, it's Tracey Munroe,' Robert said.

Emma was crying. She was staring at this woman's, this stranger's hair. It was blonde and long. It reminded her of Charly. 'Who?' she said, looking directly at Robert.

CHAPTER 62

Robert

Instead of going to work Robert rode straight to the police station. He asked to see DI Chambers and was immediately let through to his office.

'You recognised her?' DI Chambers said.

'Yes. Her name's Tracey Munroe. I went to school with her. At Parks Mead. She was in the same class as me for three years, we went on a date once. I took her to the cinema, but she didn't like the film and moaned about it all the way home. I found her quite boring to be honest. All the lads liked her. I think it was the hair.' Robert pushed an errant 'lock away from his face.

He continued. 'Personally, I got on better with the alternative crowd.' Robert smiled at this. The friendships he had made in the following years had shaped him.

'I'm not even sure why I asked her out...She died. In a car accident about a few months later. I think her dad had been driving. He was drunk and had picked her up after a party. I was too busy going to gigs at that point. I never used to be into the school party scene. I think her dad was charged, but I don't know whether he went to prison or anything.'

DI Chambers was meticulously making notes. He asked some supplementary questions. What year was this? What class? Was there anyone interested in Tracey who she had spurned? Anything else he could remember? But Robert couldn't think of anything else. School hadn't been that important to him. He'd forgotten what happened during those long, boring days. He'd spent most of his time doodling on the covers of his books. Adding detail to the pictures of the various bands he liked which he'd plastered his books with.

CHAPTER 63

DI Chambers

When he arrived at the office on Wednesday morning, there was a note stuck on his desktop. *DCI Jackson requests you meet him at 10am.* James guessed that he wanted an update. He had an hour to get a report ready. He'd make sure every small detail was documented.

DCI Jackson trusted him to be thorough and precise. Since they'd let the Superintendent go in the last round of cuts, DCI was the highest Stanton station detective rank. James did all the investigative work and DCI Jackson did the assigning, statistics and moaning when things didn't go to plan.

Hopefully, the new lead would placate him. Leave James then free to get on with the job. The second murder had raised the stakes. Expectations and hopes for an arrest were forcing everyone's hand.

No more murders. That was the bottom line.

James gathered his files and walked the short distance to DCI Jackson's office. He knocked the door and waited.

DCI Jackson boomed, 'Come in.'

As James sat down, the DCI said, 'Coffee? My wife's Sarah's bought me one of those posh coffee machines with pods. Let's see what we've got.' He placed a swivel stand of brightly coloured pods on the table. 'Caramel latte, dark espresso…?'

'I'm fine, sir. Thanks.' James brushed some imaginary lint off his trousers.

'James. I've told you before. Just call me Dave in the office.'

'Yes, sir.' James shuffled forward in his seat and placed a

manila folder on the desk. 'Here's my latest report on the Dean - Porter case, sir. Would you like me to direct you to the relevant parts?'

'I said…Oh, never mind. That won't be necessary. I will read it later.'

James waited hoping that DCI Jackson would get to the reason he'd called him in.

He didn't have to wait too long. 'James, we have a problem. I'm getting flak from the Chief about the case. If we don't get some movement soon, preferably an arrest then I might need to bring someone else in from the region. Someone with more experience of these…erm…type of cases.'

James knew he was the best local detective. They had some equally good detectives across the region, but he didn't believe that he was surpassed in terms of his intellectual abilities. He had to show he had it covered. 'We've had some new information. I'm confident that we're closer to finding the killer. Every piece of evidence brings us nearer. It's only a matter of time, sir.'

DCI Jackson sighed, 'Time is something we don't have, James. We can't afford another murder.'

Another murder. Another one, No, we couldn't afford that. Another child simply could not die.

CHAPTER 64

DI Chambers

This was the biggest case DI Chambers had ever led. He never spent time considering this. Up until now. He realised that his boss was partially right. This was the only double child killing that he had handled. But statistically how many senior officers across the country had? A multiple child murder was a rare event.

The closest he had got to anything similar was the family slaughter carried out by an estranged father. He would never forget the child's bodies that were found lying in their beds. Their father had shot them a number of times with his shotgun. Then he'd covered them with their brightly coloured duvets. Tucked them up, ready for sleep. He had stabbed their mother soon after. When he had completed his mission, he'd shot himself. It wasn't the hardest crime to solve.

They needed a breakthrough in this case. Tracey Munroe might be the key. They needed to find out all they could about her too short life. He would assign officers to the task at Wednesday's briefing. In the meantime, he'd request the files for the car accident. They would need to trace her father. See what life he had led after her death. Whether he had ever forgiven himself.

CHAPTER 65

Emma

The next day, Emma woke early. Tears fell. Silently, she sobbed. Biting her tongue. Knowing the tears wouldn't stop. Today Charly would have been seven.

Seven could have meant she was too old. Too old to be taken. The murderer may have passed her over for someone else. Seven.

At her last birthday, they had bought helium balloons emblazoned with large number sixes. The cake was in the shape of a horse's head and her Nan had secretly booked her lessons. Riding lessons. Emma remembered her face when she opened the envelope. How she'd jumped up and down, even allowing her Nan a hug and a kiss. She'd pretended she was riding around the room. Her hair swinging from side to side like a palomino's mane. Overjoyed.

Her six and seven year old friends arrived shortly after and they'd raced around. Barely sitting to play pass the parcel. Mostly boys. Screaming and screeching. Charly in the centre. The birthday girl. Smiling.

Today, they had bought flowers and a soft, plush horse.

Emma knew they were sitting on the hall table. Ready to go to the churchyard. She wondered if Robert would come with them. He never visited the grave. She normally had to go with her mum. Her mum who just sobbed the whole time.

Seven.

CHAPTER 66

Robert

Robert faced the wall. He awoke early. Knowing. He sensed Emma sobbing next to him. There were no words of comfort. What could he say? If he held her, he would shatter. He needed his strength. He needed to face another demon.

The only day he had seen Charly's grave was at the funeral. Then it was a hole that a tiny coffin was lowered into. A hole dug by melancholic men, knowing who would lie there. It had been enough for Robert. The thought that his daughter lay there under the soil made it a place he couldn't see. He just couldn't.

But he knew it hurt Emma. Why couldn't he be strong for her? Why couldn't he comfort his wife? He turned to her. She looked small and helpless. Empty and broken. He bit his lip and held her close.

'Will you come?' she asked. Her head nestled in his chest.

'Yes.' He held her tighter. Not yet knowing if his answer was truthful. He needed to find the strength.

Every birthday would be the same. He knew that. Every birthday there would be new traditions. New sadness. They'd count the years.

Today she would be seven.

They would imagine what she would have been doing if she lived. Today she would have a shiny, new bike and would ride it around the park. Her blonde hair billowing behind her. She'd imagine she was Laura Trott racing circuits. Getting faster and faster on each revolution.

Robert actually smiled at this. He held Emma tightly.

Considered telling her this story. Maybe later. If he was strong enough.

CHAPTER 67

Emma

Emma's mother arrived at twelve on the dot. She wore black. She had been crying. Her mascara was smudged, and she held a tissue tightly in her grasp. 'I got a taxi. I couldn't drive,' she sobbed.

Emma and Robert stared at her. Emma wondered if she should be crying harder. It felt like she should. That it was a crying competition with no prize.

'Don't take your jacket off. We're leaving now.' Robert took control.

Emma was relieved. She picked up the flowers and toy horse. The horse was similar to one that her mum had bought her as a child. A well-filled, tapestry-covered stuffed animal with plastic eyes. Quite ugly really. But it felt soft and comforting.

They walked to the church, it wasn't far. A sombre procession. No one spoke. They walked arm in arm. Three abreast.

The street was unusually quiet. They were only passed by a tall, older man. Emma imagined him doffing his hat in reverence, but his head was uncovered.

Then she imagined Charly skating down the street. Laughing and giggling. Maybe falling over. Getting up. Brushing herself down. Not a tear. Emma must not cry. She must smile like her daughter. She held on to Robert's arm. He was staring ahead at the churchyard.

Turning into the gate, Emma stumbled. Robert's grasp tightened. She looked up at his face. It was full of concern and something else. Fear. He looked petrified.

'Mum, you go ahead,' Emma said.

Her mum walked ahead a few paces and sat down on a bench.

Emma turned to Robert. 'This isn't her. She has gone. But it is a place we can talk to her. That's what I do.'

His eyes were darting about. Uncertainty bled from him. Emma wanted to hold him tight and say *don't do it then if you can't.* But she knew he'd regret it.

Emma continued. 'We can speak to her separately, if that helps. You can go first. I'll sit on the bench with mum.'

'What will I say?' Robert's voice was shaky and timid.

Emma smiled. 'You'll know what to say.'

As he moved away, Emma went to sit on the bench. She didn't give him directions. He knew where the grave was. She watched him, head bowed walk towards their daughter's resting place. Her mum held her hand. They sat on the bench in silence, with the flowers and the horse placed next to them.

CHAPTER 68

Robert

Robert reached Charly's grave too soon. The black granite shone as though polished by the sun. He didn't read the date or the description. Instead he rubbed the plastic doll he had in his pocket. Charly's Bat Girl.

He sat down in the grass. It was damp. But he barely noticed. 'Your mum thinks that I should talk to you, but you're not really here. I know that.'

He wouldn't look down at the grave it made it more absurd. He continued to talk to his baby girl, 'I miss you every day. That goes without saying. I miss your laughter. I miss watching you ride your rusty bike in the park and playing on the swings. Remember that day when you flew so high that you got scared that you might whizz round the top of the swing? How we'd laughed when you calmed down. We're okay, Charly. Me and your mum. Just okay. But that's better than it was a few months back.'

He didn't want to look at the gravestone, so he stared at the teddy that sat beneath it. He was about to speak again when he noticed that it was holding something. He leaned forward and picked it up. The bear was posable, and its hands were clasped together. Robert prised them apart. They held a small clump of golden hair. Charly's hair?

CHAPTER 69

Emma

Emma approached the grave holding her mum's hand. She felt like a child again. It had always just been her and mum. She never met her dad. He left before she was born. Didn't want the responsibility of a daughter. It was what had convinced her that she would find the right man, get married and then have children. Robert was the right man. She had always known that. Watching him kneeling at the grave of his daughter made her heart ache.

Emma noticed him put something into his pocket. She guessed it was Charly's Bat Girl doll. He could never give it up. It was probably the right thing to do. There'd been so many robberies of children's graves. It made Emma sad.

She walked over to Robert. Her mum took the flowers from her hand and placed them on Charly's grave. Emma knelt next to Robert putting her arms gently around him. Hugging him. She felt so cold despite it being a warm June afternoon. She watched her mum empty the vase at the foot of the gravestone of dried, dead flowers. Then she helped her arrange the new ones. 'That's better isn't it Charly.' The red and yellow daisies stood proudly. 'Your favourite colours. Happy Birthday.'

'Perhaps we should have brought a cake,' Emma's mum said.

'I couldn't eat any.' Robert said. 'I didn't wish her happy birthday. I should have done…'

Emma touched his back, 'You can say what you want. It all helps. Don't worry.'

She wondered if it made any difference to him, like it did for her. Maybe she was the daft one. Wasting her time.

Placing her hand on the granite, Emma said, 'Happy Birthday, beautiful angel. Love you to the moon and back.' She blew her a kiss and then stood. She took the horse from her mother's hands and placed it next to the teddy that was sitting in front of the gravestone looking lost. 'Look Charly. A horse for you to ride the clouds on.'

They all stood together and linked arms again. Ready for the journey home. Emma turned her head as she left the graveyard. She sensed someone was behind them but did not spot anyone. What did it matter? There must be plenty of mourners, plenty of grave talkers.

CHAPTER 70

W

He watched them leave. He had arrived early that morning, so he wouldn't miss them. He knew they would come today. They would speak to their daughter. Bring fresh flowers. Maybe toys. He'd stood in the shadows and heard the whispered 'Happy Birthday.'

He hoped they appreciated his gift. Wasn't he thoughtful.

The Wig Maker walked back to Charly's grave and picked up the horse. He raised it to his face and smelled it. So, this was Emma's sweet scent. One day he would be that close to her that he would smell it firsthand. Of this, he had no doubt.

CHAPTER 71

Robert

Robert walked home with his head down. He held Emma's hand. It felt soft against his calloused palm. He didn't want to look at the park as he passed it. The park, where memories played like an old, family video. He looked the other way. Couldn't bear a re-run of Charly's first attempt to ride a bike.

His other hand was in his jacket pocket stroking the fine blond hairs. They couldn't belong to Charly could they? This must be someone's sick idea of a joke. Or a coincidence of some kind. Maybe a child had held the teddy while her parent had visited another grave and somehow the hair got caught.

But that was ridiculous. It could never happen. Robert knew where the hair had come from. There was only one person who would have it. The thought chilled him. This was a gift from the killer. A birthday gift for the parents.

He felt nauseous and walked more quickly. In a rush now to get home.

'Slow down,' Emma whispered. 'Mum can't keep up.'

Should he tell her? If he told Emma, then she would want him to give the hair to the police. Get it tested. They would shove it into a plastic envelope and take it from him. He'd never touch it again.

He had to keep quiet. His thumb and finger rolled the hair in his pocket. Keeping it safe.

He could put it in a locket and give it to Emma for Christmas. He could say that he found it attached to the pink hairband and had kept it. It would be a beautiful surprise.

Then he realised that it had been in the hands of the killer. He had cut it from his daughter's scalp. He had touched it. Robert pulled his hand from his pocket repulsed.

When he reached home, Robert found a crisp white envelope in the kitchen drawer. He carefully placed the hair in it. He went upstairs and found his old, battle-scarred leather jacket. It smelled of mosh pits and dry ice. He placed the envelope in one of the pockets and hung it back in the wardrobe.

He didn't need to decide what to do with the hair today.

CHAPTER 72

w

The Wig Maker sat at his desk in the spare room. He opened one of the drawers in his hobby chest. In a small plastic envelope were a few of Samantha's hairs. He wondered what he would do with these. What a wonderful gift they would make for the Porters.

It filled him with pleasure watching Robert finding his gift. He guessed that he wouldn't hand them over to the police. Robert would keep them and touch them every day as he had. Getting some small joy from their softness and beauty.

CHAPTER 73

DI Chambers

The briefing started promptly at 10am on Wednesday. The Crime Scene Manager announced at the start that after due deliberation she intended to treat Mike Deyton's car as a crime scene. She was planning to have it brought in that afternoon as soon as the paperwork was completed and signed off. If DI Chambers was so inclined, he'd have marked that off as a point to him. Instead he didn't register any outward response.

Then DS Khapor spoke. 'We've always assumed because of the location of the tree that the bodies were bought to the car park. I'm wondering if that's the case. We've only traced Mike Deyton's car as a possible for Samantha's murder. We didn't trace any car for Charly's that wasn't later ruled out. What if he entered the forest from the back? We know the Deans did, so it's certainly possible. There must be an obvious place to park out of site of the road. Maybe when he hadn't been seen for Charly's murder, he got cockier with Samantha's and just used the front car park entrance or maybe he wanted to be quicker. It would take a long time getting the body through the forest.'

Janet said, 'It would be very difficult getting CCTV in that area after the length of time since Charly's murder. It's worth looking at though. The more evidence we have, the more likely it is that the killer is local. I'm happy for now that we treat the car as a possible crime scene for both murders.'

The Chief Scene of Crime Officer, Rebecca Hastings, agreed and stated that she would make examination of the car a priority. DS Khapor agreed to call Robert Dean after the meeting to find out where he had parked his bike when he went to the forest.

DI Chambers stood up when Janet Taylor had finished. The biggest task today had to be to trace Tracey Munroe's family and classmates. He quickly assigned DS Khapoor and DC Anne Black with the task. They had both been former pupils at Parks Mead and would know some of the teachers and pupils there. Neither of them were young enough to have been pupils at the same time as Tracey though.

Then Rebecca Hastings reported that they were now seventy-five per cent certain that the knife used to kill Samantha was not the exact same knife that was used to kill Cindy. She showed numerous slides that showed various cuts to bone and skin. Both knives were described as commonly used kitchen knives with serrated blades. She then went on to show comparisons of two injuries, one from each girl, and highlighted the similarities and differences. DI Chambers always appreciated how the Chief Scene of Crimes Officer always prefaced her remarks with *you must realise forensic science deals with probabilities not certainties.* In this case it seemed that the perpetrator went out to buy a new knife or used a different, previously bought, knife for each murder. The fact that these were commonplace probably wouldn't help the case unless he had kept them and traces of blood from the victims were found on them.

DI Chambers thanked Rebecca and bought the case briefing to a close. It was now 12:30pm and it was going to be another busy, long day.

CHAPTER 74

Emma

'How did you know Tracey Munroe?' Emma asked, watching Robert's face for an answer.

They were eating breakfast outside. It was still unnaturally hot for early June. Robert was surprised it had taken her so long to ask. He took another bite of toast before he answered, 'She was in the year below me at school. I didn't know her that well. We did go out...once...on a date. We went to see The Matrix. To be honest, the film was more interesting than she was.'

He blushed as he spoke. He wasn't sure why he felt so uncomfortable. He picked up a small metal watering can, ducked it in the water butt and started to water the plants. Avoiding Emma's inquiring gaze.

'I don't care that you went out. I just don't get it!' Emma had started to shout. 'What has this woman got to do with Charly?'

'She's dead.' Robert said, bluntly.

'I know Charly's...'

'I'm talking about Tracey. She died. Years ago. In a car crash.'

'So, what has that to do with us? Were you with her in the car?'

'No, this was months after we went out.'

'I don't get it!'

Emma got up without warning, stormed inside and slammed the kitchen door. Robert carried on watering the plants. He guessed Emma wanted to be on her own. She always avoided confrontation. Surely, she didn't blame him. It couldn't be his fault, could it?

CHAPTER 75

Robert

Robert was running late for work. He was filtering down Cross Road when a car started to pull out in front of him. Robert pressed his horn and the car came to a juddering halt. Robert was able to stop just behind the car's bonnet. He swore in his helmet. The car driver waved a 'sorry' and drove off allowing Robert to continue his journey. By the time he arrived at work he was fuming.

Mariam was in the office alone. She smiled when Robert walked in. 'Everyone's running late, there was a crash on Hastings Road. It's your lucky day. You might even have time for a cuppa before you get on the road.'

So, he needn't have rushed. Robert sighed, no longer angry, and sat down. Mariam's tea was the best in the city. Always strong and sweet. She even had biscuits. One of those selection packs with bourbons and pink wafers. This made up for the interrupted breakfast. When Emma had started talking, that morning, he hadn't bothered to finish his toast. He wanted to forget, at least for the rest of the day, that it might all be his fault. All his fault.

Mariam was speaking, he'd been so lost in his own thoughts that he'd missed the first bit of what she said. He just heard, '...she was wondering if you fancied going out one night.'

'Who?' Robert said, forgetting he had a mouthful of biscuit and nearly chocking.

'My cousin Nadiah. She works on the checkout at Asda. She's been trying to get Emma to go to a gig with her, but to no avail. I think she thinks that you might be able to persuade her. I said I'd ask, but this has been my first opportunity. You lot are always rushing out in the morning leaving me here with the phone and the filing.'

'Nadiah's your cousin?'

'Yes, my cousin sister. Small world I know. But you know what us Bangladeshis are like.'

'I didn't mean that.'

'I know. Anyway, Wild Mad Dog, or something like that, are playing at the Colly next Friday, so she was wondering if you wanted to go. She can get you in on the door, as her mate works in the Box Office.'

'Ferocious Dog?'

'Yes, that was it. Shall I just say yes, and you can sort it out with Emma?'

'OK, thanks,' Robert said. Maybe this was what Emma needed. A night out.

CHAPTER 76

DI Chambers

DI Chambers was sitting at his desk. He knew that the work that he had assigned would be well underway. He trusted each individual to do their job to the best of their ability. They occasionally let him down, but not often.

There was a knock on his door. It was DS Khapor. He didn't wait to be asked to come in. This occasionally bothered James, but he liked his urgency over the case.

'These reports have just arrived. You requested them, sir so I thought I'd hand them to you first,' DS Khapor's brow was furrowed. He was perhaps a little cross that the reports hadn't come to him or Anne first, since they were labelled David Munroe, the father of Tracey.

'Thanks. I requested them before the briefing.' James hoped that DS Khapor would accept that as an explanation and move on. 'I'll scan read them and get them straight to you after.'

He had said that with authority. He was the highest-ranking officer after all. He was wondering why there were two files and couldn't wait for DS Khapor to leave so he could read them.

'Sir.' DS Khapor left the office and slammed the door. Clearly still a little annoyed. He was probably going to tell DC Black what a controlling boss he was.

James opened the first file. It was a report of the car crash that killed Tracey and left her father with serious injuries.

The accident had occurred on the corner of Slater Road at around 2am on a Friday night. The car had missed the curve completely and ploughed into a barrier on the opposite side of the road. Tracey, as the passenger, had taken the brunt of the crash. Her father had hit the windscreen with some force, he hadn't been wearing a seatbelt. He had been unconscious for most of the time.

Tracey had died soon after reaching the hospital. She had a number of injuries, including head and chest. The accident and emergency staff had tried to perform a thoracotomy to release the blood in her chest wall, but it was too late.

The police had requested a blood alcohol test on her father. It came back as 230mg per 100ml blood, which was well above the legal limit.

The other piece of information that grabbed his attention was the search for a witness. A young man had been seen speaking to Tracey as she lay dying in the wreckage. He had squeezed between the bars and passenger seat. He left as soon as the ambulance arrived. No one had been able to trace him. It wasn't clear if he'd witnessed the crash. As the case was likely to go to court, the officers had gone to great lengths to try and trace him. He was described as an older teenager by witnesses. Someone of roughly Tracey's age.

The witnesses were not needed to prosecute David Munroe in the end. He had pleaded guilty. The judge banned him from driving for a year and gave him a fine of £250, believing he had suffered enough.

James opened the second file. This chronicled the investigation into the death of David Munroe. He had returned to driving shortly after his ban. Three years ago, he had been involved in a car accident. He had swerved to miss a car racing down a narrow country lane. His car had hit a tree and since he wasn't wearing a seatbelt he had died instantly. They hadn't managed to find the other car driver. He or she hadn't stopped at the scene. There were no witnesses, no paint on David's car suggesting a glancing blow and no hope of finding the driver. The only evidence that there was another car was the tyre skid marks on the road.

Some might say that this was a fitting end to the life of

David Munroe. James didn't think that. David had not had the happiest of times between killing his daughter and his death. His occupation was listed as unemployed. His previous job had been an accountant for the largest firm in Stanton. His marital status was listed as divorced. Not surprising. There wouldn't be many women who would stay with their husband after their actions had resulted in their daughter's death.

Who was the mysterious witness to Tracey's death and the speeding driver? James had a feeling in his gut that knowing the identities of both was important. But if it was difficult finding them then, it would be impossible now.

CHAPTER 77

Emma

It was lunchtime and Emma was eating a sandwich at the small table in the back room of the book shop. Her mobile started to vibrate. Emma put down her sandwich, wiped the crumbs from her hands on her trousers and picked up the phone. It was a text from Robert: *I've said we would go to see Ferocious Dog on Friday with Nadiah xxx*

She really didn't know what to think. She hadn't seen a band live since that night. She'd thought she could never go again. She'd had a row with Robert that morning and this is how he'd decided to make up! Was he that thoughtless?

But he knew Ferocious Dog were one of her favourite bands. They'd never played Stanton before, so this was a first. They hadn't thought twice about travelling to other cities in the past. They'd arranged for her mum to babysit and often travelled with Robert's dad in his van. They'd even slept on friend's floors to keep the cost down. But things were different now.

By not going to gigs they'd lost all those friends. They weren't the sort that would know what to say. Those friends had not spoken, texted, emailed or contacted them on Facebook. They'd simply ignored them when Charly was killed. The things that bought them together — the music, the gigs — had in the last six months shown they were no real ties. Emma wasn't sure she wanted to see them, but she did desperately miss the music, the dancing and the singing along. She picked up her sandwich again and carried on eating. Not replying to Robert's text.

CHAPTER 78

DI Chambers

Sara Mason, one of the police officers assigned to the murder investigation team tapped on his office door. She was waiting patiently for him to tell her to enter, clutching and unclutching her hands.

Was he that scary? He wondered, as he asked her to come in. She sat down but didn't start speaking straight away.

'I had a thought,' she said. 'So, I checked it out.'

'Go on,' DI Chambers urged.

She was staring at the photograph of his family on his desk. It seemed to help her compose herself.

'I thought there might be a link between the supermarket and the school. So, I checked. There is someone. One of the security guards. His name is Joshua Cummins. He was in the same year as Robert Dean.'

DI Chambers smiled. He had already checked this himself, but it was good to see that someone on the team was willing to show some initiative.

'Did you check if he's working today, by any chance?' he said.

'Yes, and he is,'

'Why don't we go and pick him up then,'

DI Chambers stood up and they left his office together. He saw Sarah blushing as she walked across the incident room. He wanted her on the main team and hoped that she would feel proud and not embarrassed. DI Chambers stood at the front of the incident room and announced that they were heading to Asda to pick up a suspect.

He then arranged two teams and briefed them as to where in proximity to the supermarket he wanted them positioned. He gave a copy of a risk assessment he had written to each team leader and highlighted the main exit points. He didn't seem to think that they would have too much trouble arresting the suspect. The hope was for a quick — go in and handcuff as quickly as possible. What they didn't want was for the suspect to return home. Sara thought must have thought it was odd that DI Chambers had already completed a risk assessment for the arrest, copied a full-scale floor plan of the supermarket and obtained a search warrant for Joshua's flat. She didn't say anything though, she was just looked pleased that she had been put on the main arrest team.

CHAPTER 79

DI Chambers

As DI Chambers drove to the supermarket he considered the evidence. He knew that the link between the school and the supermarket was at best tenuous. He knew that without the pressure, without the media calling for blood and the threats of removal from the case, he might take more time.

But it had to be done. If he removed the threat to another child. If he asked the right questions, found extra evidence then it would be worth the fishing expedition.

What was he becoming? One of those coppers he hated. That would do anything for an arrest. That didn't much care if they were right. If the evidence stuck even in the short term that was enough. But it wasn't. Not really. Not for DI Chambers. He had to get it right.

He could turn the car round. Call off the troops. But they might learn something. And if it was the killer then the next victim would be saved. James knew the killer would be stalking again. Would be seeking another girl with long blonde hair or had found one. Would be waiting for the opportunity to remove her from her home, from her loving family. Taking her, murdering her, stabbing her and scalping her.

DI Chambers fought his doubts. Brushed them away. It was better that they picked up the suspect. It could be him. It could be the security guard, Josh Cummins.

CHAPTER 80

Nicole

Nicole was picking up yet more baby supplies as the police cars pulled up outside Asda. She stood waiting for the cashier to remove the security tag from the bag of nappies. She never understood why they tagged them. She always thought if mothers were so hard up that they needed to steal nappies, then good luck to them. She looked down at Rosie in her pushchair. Rosie was biting on one of her plastic toys. She was teething again.

Nicole watched as the DI strode up to one of the security guards. She knew it was the inspector in charge of the murders of those two poor young girls, as she had seen him on the news. Without any fuss, the uniformed police placed the security guard in handcuffs and led him away to the police cars parked at the entrance.

Nicole looked down at Rosie in the pushchair who was giggling at the woman waiting in the checkout line pulling silly faces at her. Nicole would have taken her out of the pushchair there and then and given her a huge hug, but she knew how hard it would be to get her back in the pushchair after. She would wait until she got home. She guessed that every mother in the country must have that same reaction whenever they thought of those poor girls.

As she pushed the pushchair towards the exit, Nicole overheard the cashiers. *I knew there was something odd about him. I told you didn't I!* If it was this guy maybe that would explain the strange feelings she'd been having. She shuddered, pushing Rosie a little faster out of the shop.

CHAPTER 81

Emma

Emma always switched on the news when she arrived home from work. It didn't matter what shift she was doing, she would go straight to the news channel, just in case. Five minutes in and the news presenter announced: *there has been a development in the Charlotte Dean and Samantha Porter murder case. A 27-year-old man is helping police with their enquiries. He is believed to live and work locally.*

Robert walked in a few moments later. Emma was still staring at the television screen constantly rewinding with the remote to listen to those three sentences again and again. They both stood there stunned.

Patrice ended their paralysis by knocking on the front door.

'Sorry, I tried to get here sooner, but the traffic is terrible. I take it you've heard,' Patrice said as soon as she'd sat down in the same place she always sat, their only armchair. Emma and Robert sat on the settee facing her.

'Do we know him?' Robert asked.

Emma winced at this. The mere thought that it could be someone they knew. Although, it was more likely someone Robert knew. Someone he went to school with.

Patrice was giving nothing away. 'I'm sorry, until it's agreed that I can tell you who we have, which isn't likely to happen until after he is charged, then I can't tell you anything about him.'

'He's local though, isn't he? They said so in the press,'

Robert insisted. 'You must know who he is. I don't know why you can't tell us. Surely you trust us by now. We've never spoken to the papers.'

'It's not up to me. I don't make the rules,' Patrice replied.

'Then why are you here. Maybe you should leave,' Robert stood up.

Patrice unflustered said, 'I'm here to keep you informed of as much as the investigation as I can. As soon as I'm told that I can divulge the name of the suspect I will. Now if you still need me to leave...'

'Will you come back and tell us his name,' Emma said biting her lip. She was sitting on the sofa hugging her knees. Patrice was staring at her. No doubt sensing how ill she felt. She desperately wanted Patrice to leave so she could cry, scream, let the pain out.

'Of course, the very moment I'm given permission I will come round,' Patrice stood up to go, not meeting Robert's eye, but smiling reassuringly at Emma.

After Patrice had left, Robert went up to Emma and hugged her. 'It's good news isn't it,' he said.

'I don't want to see him. I don't want to see the monster,' Emma said, pressing her face into Robert's shoulder. She knew that she would have to face this demon at some point but, whereas, Robert wanted the chance to gain some retribution, some vengeance, some justice; she just wanted to have some peace, some escape, some divorce from the horror.

CHAPTER 82

Josh

Josh Cummins, the security guard, was placed in a cell at Stanton police station. He had been incarcerated for an hour whilst his solicitor, a friend of his aunts, could be located. He glanced around at the cold, empty cell and wondered how he came to be held here. How had he got to being placed in handcuffs, fingerprinted and photographed from every angle? How had he got to being body searched and questioned on all his medical history by a doctor he had never met before? He wasn't angry or upset, just completely numb. How on earth could they suspect him? What had he done wrong?

CHAPTER 83

DI Chambers

DI James Chambers was glad that he had a break before interviewing the suspect. It gave him the opportunity to review his notes further. It, also, meant that a team had already been dispatched to search Joshua Cummin's flat. He lived alone on Davenport Close. Close to both of the girl's houses. In fact, if you got a piece of string and placed it from one house to the other, then Joshua's flat would probably fall in the centre of it. James didn't know if this was significant, but he made a note of it.

He ran a hand through his thick, grey hair and then undid the top button of his shirt. He wrote a series of questions on his yellow legal pad. He checked off the photographs that he planned to refer to in the interview. He lingered on the two pictures of Charlotte and Samantha. The ones taken when they were alive. He wanted to spend time on these. He wanted the suspect to see them as two young girls. Girls who loved to play. Charlotte who loved adventures, who was forever emulating her hero, Bat Girl. Riding her bike too fast, climbing and jumping. Samantha, who loved animals and wanted to be a vet when she grew up.

It was very possible that this man had no remorse. That he couldn't, and would never, see these girls as children. They were just a means to get what he wanted. DI Chambers hypothesised that this was their golden hair. Why else would he have shorn them? But what did he want it for? James always waited to make assumptions until he had facts. However, he now needed to test some theories out. Theories that had been raised by members of the team in the incident room and at the case reviews. He needed to see how their suspect responded. He hadn't made his mind up that this was the killer. He wouldn't until he had all the evidence before him. All written, recorded and properly labelled.

      He called in DC Black who was going to assist him with the interview. They ran through each question and possible supplementaries. DI Chambers had always been a meticulous planner before interviews, even prior to the latest Home Office guidance. What was it called?...PEACE. Implying that interviews should be peaceful, leisurely affairs.

CHAPTER 84

Robert

Robert woke with a start. He remembered that with the revelations of the last couple of days, he had forgotten to get back in touch with Simon. He debated ringing him or going round to his house that evening. He, also, debated telling Emma and seeing whether she wanted to tag along. She was sound asleep beside him. All curled up in a ball. He noted that she had slept much better the last two nights. He hadn't found her asleep downstairs in the evenings either. He guessed that having possibly found and arrested their child's killer had led to her feeling more secure and at peace. It hadn't had that effect on him. If anything, he felt more restless. He had to keep fighting the urge to barge in to Stanton Police Station and demand to see the killer. He'd fight off any police officers that stood in his way and find the bastard, beat him to a pulp and rip out his hair.

Robert then realised he'd been beating the pillow. He looked at Emma. She was still sleeping. He decided he would go and see Simon alone that evening. Maybe he'd ring him and suggest they meet away from the women. They could meet at a pub out in the countryside. As far away from Stanton as possible. Where nobody knew them.

CHAPTER 85

Emma

Emma lay silently next to Robert, curled in a ball. In her head was her vision of what the killer looked like. A monster with eyes that bore into your soul and missing teeth. Who cackled and screeched. She knew she should be happy that they'd found Charly's killer. That would be the normal reaction.

Sharon Davies, one of the mum's she knew whose son had been murdered in a fight at the park, held a party when they arrested her son's killer. She'd got so drunk that she'd invited all the reporters in and told them wild tales of her past. Fortunately, only the worst kind of rag had printed them. The rest just concentrated on stories of the killer's childhood and his Army career.

Emma didn't understand why she always reacted differently to news than Robert. They were a couple. Why didn't they feel the same? She never tried to hide how she felt, but sometimes she couldn't explain to him, couldn't find the exact words to describe the emotions each new event elicited. He was clearly over the moon that someone was in custody. He wanted to know everything about the monster. What he really wanted was to take him by the throat and torture him.

Emma sighed and rolled away from her husband, as much as their double bed would allow. He must have noticed as he pulled her in for a hug.

'It's great news, isn't it,' he murmured in her ear.

'Ummm,' was all she could muster.

'I'm glad you're sleeping better. I can't sleep. I'd like to go round and finish the bastard off.' Robert held her more tightly. It was beginning to hurt.

Emma couldn't decide whether it was best to tell him that she couldn't sleep because all she could see was a monster's face and that she just wanted everything to be over. She knew what was to come — a court case. They'd have to sit there listening to every detail of their daughter's final hours. They'd have to look at that monster every single day, until he was convicted and what if he wasn't convicted? How would that make them feel.

In the end she just muttered, 'I'm glad they've got him,' and shut her eyes.

CHAPTER 86

DS Khapor

Sergeant Anil Khapor had finished bagging up and itemising all of the evidence they had found in Joshua Cummins' flat. He gazed at the pile of bags they had waiting for the van that would take them to the forensic science labs they used. Everything now had to be split into categories for the different private companies they outsourced to. Fortunately, this was the Crime Scene Manager and Exhibits Officer's job, not his. The CSM was finishing off in the kitchen. A uniformed officer was scrabbling around under the sink. Removing half empty bottles of bleach and floor cleaner that clearly hadn't been recently used.

The flat was a state. They had found piles of porn in the bedroom. Joshua Cummins clearly had a liking for big breasted, blonde women. Most of the magazines were folded open on these. They had collected them in bags. They also had his laptop. There was no password protection and the internet history was plain to see. When Joshua Cummins had finished eyeing up blondes, he would spend most of his time playing online poker.

DS Khapor wrote down some notes for his boss. If he left soon he might be able to hand them to him before this morning's interview. Last night, they had decided to simply concentrate on confirming the suspect's name, address and place of work. They had then asked for details of his shift patterns around the time of the disappearance of the two girls. He knew there was a team working with the supermarket manager confirming this.

Today's interview would be key. His boss had decided to take in Detective Constable Anne Black with him. Anil was feeling slightly annoyed about this, particularly since it was protocol for DSs and DCs to interview. He would have liked the opportunity to break down this evil bastard. Instead he wrote *no sign of human hair other than suspect's own in flat* in his notebook.

CHAPTER 87

DI Chambers

It was that time. DI Chambers did up his top shirt button and adjusted his tie. He had all of the evidence neatly stacked and ordered next to him. Anne Black had the same beside her. 'Are you ready Anne?' He asked and when she nodded, he requested that the suspect Josh Cummins be brought into the interview room with his solicitor.

James decided to wait for a few moments before speaking. He waited, as he wanted to spend some time having a really good look at the suspect. However, the solicitor, Steven Salt was distracting him. Steven looked uncomfortable and kept fidgeting in his chair. James was concerned that he might not be up for the job. He wanted the interview to be at least fair and hoped that if he overstepped the mark, this young solicitor would stop him in his tracks.

James looked back at Josh. He looked terrified. He was chewing the collar of his long-sleeved t-shirt and his eyes were darting all over the place trying to take it all in.

D.I. Chambers recited the PACE pre-interview speech, word for word, and pressed record on the digital recorder — stating the date, time and the names of those present. He then explained to Josh why they were questioning him, that he was merely helping with their enquiries into the deaths of Charlotte Dean and Samantha Porter. He then went down the list of confirmation questions. How old was he? What was his date of birth? What was his address? Did he have any access to other properties? Where did he work? What were his hours of work? Did he drive? What car did he drive?

There was a pause. Josh Cummins stated that he did drive and that he had a Corsa. DI Chambers and DC Anne Black excused themselves for the tape. James sent Anne to call Anil and she left the interview room. He was fortunately still at the suspect's house and he heard her ask him to check the house for car keys. Then she got one of the officers to check with the DVLA what car or cars Josh was the registered keeper of. James was annoyed, as they had him listed as driving a green Renault Clio not a Corsa. He wasn't sure where the mistake had come from. They quickly went back into the interview room. DI Chambers said, 'For the tape, can you confirm the make, model and registration of any cars you either own or have access to drive.'

'I've got a Corsa, it should be parked at work still,' Josh stammered.

'Where are the keys?' asked Anne.

'In my locker at work. You can get them if you like. The code is 1234. I know you are going to tell me that I should have something more secure, but I'm rubbish at remembering numbers,' he said, glad that they were still asking questions he could answer.

Anne nodded to the police officer by the door, who went to send someone to alert Janet Taylor that they had another possible crime scene — the Corsa in the car park at Asda.

'Did you own a Clio?'

'Yes, briefly. It had belonged to my mum. She died last year of cancer.'

'What happened to the Clio?' James continued.

'I sold it on eBay a month ago.'

James told both Josh and the solicitor that they would need the paperwork relating to the sale as soon as possible. They would need to trace it, recover and search it.

James then adjourned the interview for a twenty-minute comfort break and made a note of the time. He needed to discuss the next steps through with Anne.

CHAPTER 88

DI Chambers

Anne came into his office with two freshly-brewed coffees a few minutes later.

'What do you reckon?' she said.

'I'm not convinced it's him, but we haven't got down to specific questions about both evenings yet... Is it me Anne, or do you think that he couldn't be that good an actor. He wouldn't appear to be that frightened? I just can't see it myself. Whoever did this, took those girls - in twilight in Charly's case, practically daylight in Samantha's and nobody saw him. He killed them almost immediately and then dumped them. It would take a great deal of arrogance, confidence or downright dispassionate brutality to do that. All I can see in that interview room is a frightened child.'

'So, what are you suggesting?'

'Run through the list of questions we already have. Then we will review. We've only got a few hours left before we need to charge him. If all we get is what we've got up to now, we will just have to release him.'

Anne didn't disagree with him. She had frowned instead and bit into the side of her polystyrene coffee cup.

CHAPTER 89

Josh

Josh had asked to go to the toilet during the break. He had vomited up bile into the toilet bowl and placed his forehead against the side of the toilet cubicle. He waited until he felt his heart stop racing enough, so that he could reach for a tissue and wipe his mouth. Up until now, he could answer their questions, but he knew the next bit would be harder. What if he had no alibi that they could — what was it his solicitor had said? — corroborate. It was extremely likely. He only ever went to the gym or to the cinema to see a Disney film with his younger brother. His brother wouldn't even remember the dates, as he had global developmental delay. He lived in a care home in the next town and the only times they saw each other, was once a month for an evening or afternoon out. He thought that it was possible that the care home had a record, but what if they didn't?

The police officer that had escorted him to the toilet, started banging on the toilet door. Josh slowly rose to his feet. He left the cubicle and washed his hands under the watchful eye of the police officer, who then escorted him back to the interview room. His solicitor was still sitting there playing with his pen. Pushing the nib down, clicking it repeatedly. Whatever mess he had gotten himself in, Josh already knew this solicitor was not going to be his saviour.

CHAPTER 90

Josh

DI Chambers and DC Black returned to the interview room. As soon as she sat down, DC Black turned over a photograph. It was Charlotte Dean. Josh recognised her from the newspaper. She was wearing her school uniform and was half smiling at the camera. Josh started trembling, waiting for the question.

'Do you recognise this girl?' DI Chambers asked.

'Yes,' Josh muttered not looking at James, but still staring at the photograph. 'I saw her in the papers and on the television. It's Charlotte Dean.'

'Had you seen her before she died?' asked James.

'I think so...maybe where I work at Asda.'

'And did you know any of her family prior to this?'

'I knew her dad vaguely. We went to the same school. We weren't friends or nothing.' Josh looked at the floor, sat on his hands to try and stop them shaking. He couldn't look at either of the detectives. It made him feel guilty even though he hadn't done anything. It was always like this. If the teacher had told off the class for talking, he would be the one to blush, despite not having said a word.

Josh remembered Robert Dean. At school he had been quiet and aloof. No one ever bothered him. He knew the names of loads of alternative bands and was always boasting about the gigs he'd been to. No one else had heard of them. But he was strong and tall for his age so, unlike Josh, he was never bullied. Josh was bullied on a daily basis.

DI Chambers then showed him a photograph of Samantha Porter. She was laughing and chasing a large, black Labrador. 'Do you know who this is?' he said, pointing at the picture.

'Only from the television. She might have come in the supermarket, I dunno.'

Then came that question. 'What were you doing on Friday 11th November?'

How was he to know. It was months ago. It's not like he needed a diary. The only dates he kept on his phone were his work schedule. He shrugged.

'For the tape, Joshua Cummins shrugged his shoulders,' DC Black said.

'How am I supposed to know. It was months ago,' Josh said into his sleeve, which he was now biting again.

'Don't you think you would remember. Everyone in Stanton must remember what they were doing that day. I mean it's not every day a six-year-old is abducted and murdered,' DC Black reminded him.

He hadn't thought of it like that. He didn't know whether to scream or cry now. But then suddenly he vaguely remembered something. He'd worked all day and gone to bed early with a migraine. When he'd woken up, he'd switched on the radio and heard that a body had been found in the woods off Derbyshire Avenue.

'Wait,' he said, his voice steady for the first time in the interview, 'I'd got a migraine. I went to bed.'

'Can anyone corroborate this?' asked DI Chambers.

'No...no wait. Maria can, on the Pharmacy. I bought some Microlevel off her before I went home from my shift at 3pm. Surely, that tells you I was unwell.' He looked at his solicitor for confirmation. His solicitor just shrugged.

'What about on Friday 12th May, what were you doing on that day?' DC Black asked.

He scratched his head. Then his hand. Scratched the skin until it became a vivid red.

'I can't remember,' he said eventually.

He knew how bad that sounded. It wasn't as long

ago, but his mind was a complete blank. He remembered overhearing the checkout girls talking about the murder the next day, but he couldn't for the life of him recall what he'd done on the Friday.

The rest of the interview went in a blur. They'd shown him photographs of the dead girls. He'd started sobbing. They'd then left him alone with his solicitor who had muttered something about him not being charged yet so that was good. He just sat there in the chair completely dazed. Not knowing what the hell was going on.

CHAPTER 91

DI Chambers

Time was running out. They needed to charge him or let him go. DS Khapor had returned from the house search with nothing of much note in the way of physical evidence. Yes, Joshua Cummins liked blonde women with big breasts, but these were women not girls. They was no hair at the site or blood, or anything particularly incriminating. The only possible areas to still search were the cars and James wasn't hopeful that they would reveal much.

Josh had two cars at his disposal at the time of the murders why would he have stolen or borrowed Mike Deyton's car? Which reminded him. They hadn't got a report on that yet. He would contact the crime lab in the morning. The recent cuts at the Vehicle Investigation Lab had held up a number of investigations. He was due a meeting with DCI Jackson in the coming weeks, so he made a note, he would raise it with him then.

Two hours later, he received the news that the preliminary search of Josh's car was clean. The full forensic examination wouldn't be completed for days, but they didn't seem hopeful. The car was dirty and dusty but there were no obvious stains or blonde hairs inside the car or boot. They hadn't yet traced the car that he had sold.

James had to make that dreaded decision and release Josh Cummins without charge.

CHAPTER 92

W

The wig maker smiled as he watched the evening news. They had released Joshua Cummins, although the television reporter said that he was still 'helping the police with their enquiries'. The wig maker had guessed they wouldn't keep Josh long. He was too stupid. Too naive. There was no way that the police would see him as the killer.

The wig maker took his cup of tea upstairs. He opened the door to his spare room and admired his own handiwork. He knew he would have to wait a week or so to get some new hair. If he was meticulous in his planning, he could frame Josh and get the rest of the hair he needed. Something was stirring again within him. He could sense it rising, but he was skilled at keeping the darkness at bay. He could pull his cap down and hide in the shadows whenever he needed to. He could pause for a while and then pounce. There was no rush.

CHAPTER 93

Robert

Robert sat opposite Simon in the Weavers Pub nursing a pint of Abbots Ale. He noticed how unhealthy this fellow griever looked. All hollowed out, empty and broken. They both raised their glasses and drank a number of times before they spoke. They needed the comfort of the drink, warming their insides, giving them time to think and consider why they were here and what had happened in the last few hours.

Robert spoke first, 'I spoke to my dad. Charly's head was covered in the same way. He didn't ask though...Why that might be.'

'He must have done something to their heads,' Simon said then paused. 'Maybe that's where he hit them?'

'I don't think so. I'm sure Patrice said he stabbed Charly once in the heart. Death was immediate. I think that was supposed to be a comfort. I guess it was. I couldn't bear it if she suffered...' Robert stopped speaking. The lump was forming in his throat again. He swallowed more beer in the hope of dislodging it, not wanting to break down in front of Simon. He was supposed to be the strong one. The one further down the grief road. The one surviving and getting back his life.

Simon wasn't speaking either. He was staring into his pint. Eventually he said, 'If not the method of death, what then? Is it their hair?'

Robert thought of Charly's beautiful blonde hair. He liked it when she wore it long. She always looked uncomfortable with it dragged back into a ponytail or plaited. She was like an Amazon when her hair was long and flowing. It was her strength. When she died, and Emma emptied her room, one of the many times, she found sixty three hairbands stuffed in drawers and under the mattress. Wearing the pink hairband reminded Robert of Charly's strength. He was taking the burden of the hairband off her. It was a message of solidarity. The mere thought that the killer may have removed her strength in an act of evil, sickened Robert to the core.

'Oh god, I hope that wasn't the reason,' he said sitting on his hands. 'I just couldn't bear it.'

Simon seemed to be having similar thoughts. He was rubbing a patch on his palm. It was red raw and bleeding. It reminded Robert of the eczema his brother had suffered as a baby. He felt for Simon, but this was more than empathy, this was the knowledge that they were now brothers in grief. Both seeking revenge and justice in equal measure but having no clue how to achieve either. It was the guilt that shredded them, ravaged them and made them numb.

'Do you think the police are doing enough. You know, to catch the right killer,' Robert asked. He had never questioned the investigation before. Always assumed that DI Chambers was competent and thorough. That any evidence would be found and meticulously investigated. He was angry though that they'd arrested someone only to release them a day later.

'I don't know. If they'd got the wrong man, I'd rather they let them go,' Simon said. 'It must be worse for you though. You've had so much longer. They seem to be making more headway now that they have two.'

Simon stopped speaking and Robert realised what he had meant. Almost implying that Samantha's death had served a purpose. Made it easier for the police to find the killer. It was true, but he didn't want to consider it. He looked at Simon who was staring at the bottom of his glass.

'Shall I get them in?' Robert asked.

'Yes. This will be my last then I'd better get back to Jane. She will be wondering where I am. I only said I would be at a late meeting.'

Robert had told Emma that he was pricing up a job and would be home by eight. He was putting off going home, knowing what tomorrow would bring. He had just enough time for another one.

When he sat back down, Simon looked straight at him. 'Do you think he was stalking another girl?'

Robert sat bolt upright, knocking the side of the table so the beers shook and spilled. 'I can't think that. Jesus.'

'But you must have considered it, I know I have.' Simon took a huge gulp of his beer and wiped his face with the back of his hand.

'Yes...actually no. I can't think that.' Maybe that's what all his dreams were about, not the stalking of Charly but the stalking of another victim.

Simon stared towards the bar and sighed. 'I think about it all the time.'

'What can we do to stop him?' Robert's leg began to shake.

Simon seemed so much more composed. 'Nothing... absolutely nothing.'

CHAPTER 94

Emma

Emma walked home from the bookshop. It was a warm pleasant evening. Robert was working late pricing up a job so there was no rush to get home. Emma decided to walk along the canal. She rarely walked along the towpath. Life was such a rush. Even without Charly, she still had tea to cook or the washing up to do. If it was Robert's turn to cook, there was still washing, ironing, cleaning up and she loved to sit for an hour or two with a good book. Dreaming. Living someone else's hopes or problems.

The towpath was more overgrown than the last time she'd walked this way. There was more rubbish in the canal too. It saddened Emma. There were so few beautiful and calm spots in Stanton. It was becoming more of a large town than a semi-rural retreat. Maybe it was time to consider moving.

There was a row of canal boats ahead. Brightly painted, almost imperceptibly bobbing up and down in the water. Maybe they could buy a boat. Sail up and down the canals. She imagined Robert at the tiller. Letting her steer when they reached a lock, so he could swing the gates open. Sleeping together in a huge, softly furnished double bed with the gentle rocking of the boat. It seemed so idyllic, so far removed from reality.

One of the narrowboat doors opened and out stepped a skinny guy with dreadlocks. He had an equally skinny and scruffy Wolfhound attached to the string he held in his hand. He smiled at Emma.

Emma smiled back. She knew him. 'Rich!' She ran and

jumped on to the deck, hugging him tightly. 'I can't believe it's you. When did you get back from Bristol?'

Emma let him go and he sat down on one of the worn pillows on the deck. Rich's dog sniffed at Emma as she sat down next to him. Rich said, 'I'm so sorry about Charly. I hadn't seen the news or anything. It wasn't until I was sitting in a pub the other night and I saw her picture on the television that I found out. I only came back to Stanton three weeks ago.'

Emma shivered, 'It's okay. You're probably the only person who wouldn't know. I envy your life, Rich. I'd love to drop out of it all myself.'

'Be careful what you wish for. I lost my job as a sound engineer last month, which is why I'm back. I've now only got a roving license, so I can't even stay here long. No job and no permanent home isn't much fun.'

'But you've got your boat and this dog.' The Wolfhound had nestled his head in Emma's lap. It looked up at her with soulful eyes. 'What's his name?'

Rich blushed. 'He's a girl. I call her, Moonbeam.'

Emma punched him in the arm and smiled. 'You used to call me that when we were hanging out together.'

The blush grew and with Rich's fair colouring, was more than obvious. Emma rested her head on his shoulder. 'I miss those times.'

'So do I,' Rich said. 'But look at us now. All grown up and responsible.'

'You…responsible!' Emma laughed.

'Well I have my dog and you have…' Rich paused, realising what he was about to say. 'Robert…you have Robert.'

'Yes. I have Robert.' Emma had wanted to say *my soul mate*, but there were days when she doubted he was. 'What about you? …Found that special someone?'

'I'm such a catch…me,' Rich said. 'Come on. I'll show you around my special girl.' He stood up and took Emma's hand, leading her inside.

Emma wasn't sure what she expected. But it wasn't this.

The interior of the boat was immaculate. The floor was a dark polished oak. The living space was dominated by a white wood burner surrounded by brightly painted tiles. Every part of the interior had a purpose. Along one side was a light oak folded table. Along the other was a plaid-cushioned sofa. 'Oh my...This is stunning, Rich.'

'I know I'm a scruffy sod, but this is my pride and joy. I've spent a lot of time getting her right,' he grinned. 'Shall I make us a coffee?'

'Please.'

The kitchen space was compact. There was a range for cooking and a refrigerator. The units and worktops were made of a pale solid wood. The shapes were hand carved to fit the space. Emma stroked the wood. 'You built this, didn't you.'

'Made the kitchen?'

'Yes. You carved it yourself. It's stunning, Rich.'

'Thanks. Knew all those years hanging out in the woods would come to sommat.' He winked.

It was Emma's turn to blush. They'd shared many a bottle of cider at local festivals. Hanging out in the woods. This was before she met Robert and was entirely innocent. They were just good friends. The best of friends. Emma often wondered what would have happened if they'd actually got together. But then she wouldn't have Robert and she wouldn't have had Charly.

Time sped by. Drinking coffee and reminiscing. Remembering old friends. Wild days and crazy nights. It was time to leave — all too soon.

'I want to get back before Robert...I'd better go.' Emma stood.

Rich stood too, closely followed by Moonbeam, who hadn't had her evening walk. 'I'll see you out and take you part of the way home, if you like.'

'Don't worry yourself. I'll be fine.' Emma didn't turn to look at Rich as she left. She wasn't sure what she would do if he tried to hug her.

'You take care now. D'you hear?' She heard him say as

she walked along the towpath. She raised her hand, turned and waved. He was dragging Moonbeam on her string, in the opposite direction.

As she walked under the bridge and up the path to the main road, Emma felt her hair prickle. She turned and peered back under the bridge. She thought she saw a shadow slinking back against the concrete joist. She wasn't sure though. It could be her imagination. She picked up her pace. Anxious to get home.

CHAPTER 95

W

The Wig Maker sat on his black, mock leather sofa eating crackers and cheddar. He didn't much care where the crumbs were going. Tonight had been amusing. Watching Emma with that scruffy hippie was a joy. She looked more than ready to do the dirty on Robert. Maybe that's what they were doing on the boat. Having cheap sex.

Luscious Emma being unfaithful. How delicious. He took another bite of cracker. A fresh layer of crumbs landed on his trousers. He brushed them onto the floor.

Robert deserved to be broken. To have his life shattered by adultery. He'd left Tracey to die. She'd even called out his name in the wreckage. He had held her hand as the blood drained from her body and for some reason, she thought that he was Robert. He was the only one who truly loved Tracey. Why would any woman want a crusty, dreadlocked hippie anyway? What did they see in them? Dirty, smelly unwashed hair. Disgusting.

One day he might scalp Robert of his 'locks. The thought made the Wig Maker laugh out loud, spraying more crumbs from his open mouth.

Perhaps he should tell Robert of his wife's indiscretion. He could send him a text or an email. But he wasn't computer savvy enough for it not to be traced. He didn't take stupid risks, it could wait. He would have to think of another way of letting him know.

CHAPTER 96

Emma

It was good seeing Rich again. It reminded Emma that there were alternatives. She didn't have to stay in Stanton. She could take off.

She stirred the vegetable stew. Robert would be home soon. It was just after eight.

Of course, she couldn't leave Stanton. Not until the killer was caught. Not until they had closure. Emma hated that word. Closure. Just shut the door on your grief. It's all over now. Life can go back to normal. The killer has been caught and put behind bars. Draw a line under it.

As if you could ever draw a line under your daughter's death.

Emma felt guilty. She was happy sitting on the narrowboat with Rich. Dreaming about life, chugging up and down the canals. She'd imagined herself reading on the sofa, watching ducks swim past her window. Moonbeam lying at her feet. The heat glowing from the wood burner. Watching it's flames. Leaning against Rich… No, she couldn't think that. She loved Robert.

Nothing had happened. She would tell Robert that she'd met Rich as soon as he came in.

Or perhaps not. Perhaps she wouldn't tell him anything at all. Nothing had happened.

CHAPTER 97

Robert

Emma had made vegetable stew. It needed more salt, but Robert didn't say. He didn't want to upset her.

'Did you have a good day at the bookshop?' he asked, spearing a carrot.

Emma looked up at him, 'Just the usual. Did you get any business tonight?'

Tonight? He'd forgotten that he'd told Emma that he was pricing up a job. 'Probably, we'll find out later.'

As soon as they'd eaten, Robert took the plates into the kitchen to wash up. He expected Emma to pick up a book and read, but she followed him.

She stood next to him at the sink. Looking worried. 'I bumped into Rich today. At the canal. He's back in Stanton. He has this crazy hound called Moonbeam of all things.'

Rich…Robert couldn't remember him, at first. Guessed he must be the one with the boat. He only knew a few of Emma's friends before they got together. They were all into music, magic mushrooms and festivals. Pretty much like himself apart from the mushrooms. He hated drugs. Didn't like how they made him feel.

Emma continued. 'It was good seeing him. Hadn't seen him in years. You should see his boat. It's stunning.'

Robert added the washing up liquid to the water in the bowl. 'You might as well dry — standing there.'

Emma reached for a tea towel, carried on talking about Rich, his dog and his boat. Then she said, 'Do you ever think of leaving Stanton?'

Robert paused. Dropping a mug back into the bowl. Soapy water splashed over the edge. 'No…sometimes I think about getting on my bike and riding and not stopping. Does that count?'

'I guess. One day, I'd like to live by the sea…'

'When we're retired. Isn't that everyone's dream. Then they realise that they don't have the hips and knees for coastal walks.'

'Don't spoil it.' Emma smiled.

'Are you sure you don't want to live on a barge with what's-his-face?'

'No!' Emma splashed him with the bubbles.

Robert hoped that wasn't the case.

Emma took Robert's arm. 'Let's forget this. It can wait until the morning.'

Robert knew what was coming. He'd much rather be making love than washing up, so he let himself be led by Emma. He wasn't concerned about Rich. He was with Emma. Rich was all alone with the dog with the funny name.

CHAPTER 98

Emma

Emma lay in Robert's arms. Traced the Celtic tattoo on his arm. Re-painting each swirl with her finger. He loved her. He didn't have to say. It was obvious. She was lucky to have him.

Guilt. That's what she felt tonight. She'd spent the evening thinking about another man. How could she even be unfaithful in her mind.

Robert's chest softly rose and fell as he slept. But Emma couldn't sleep. Robert always slept like a baby after they had sex. Emma always lay awake. Their response always opposite. Always different. It hadn't bothered Emma until now. She wanted to shake him awake and tell him, 'I thought about leaving with Rich, about sailing away and leaving you.' She may well have said that she wanted to leave him and Charly.

She rolled over away from Robert. She didn't deserve him tonight. Didn't deserve his love, his comfort, his tender touch. She was an unfaithful wife…in her head. The place where it mattered the most.

CHAPTER 99

Emma

Emma walked to work the next morning along the tow path. Hoping, expecting to see Rich. She walked past his boat. The curtains were drawn and the door leading to the deck tightly shut.

Emma didn't stop and knock. Just slowed her pace. It was 8:30 in the morning. Rich was a sound engineer, a night worker not a day slaver. Of course, he was still asleep. What was she thinking?

As soon as she walked past the boat, Emma's pace quickened, and she pushed all thoughts of Rich and Moonbeam out of her head.

Tonight, she was going out for the first time in ages. That's what she needed to think about not old friends and ridiculous fantasies. What was she doing? Her and Rich…a childhood dream.

CHAPTER 100

Emma

It was after 6pm on a Friday. Emma was getting ready to go out. She wore the New Model Army Green and Grey tee shirt and a pair of black combats. She couldn't decide whether to wear her trusty, old Doc Martens or the clogs she bought in the eighties at a festival. She decided on the Docs as they were easier to dance in. She wrapped the clogs in tissue paper, placed them back in a shoe box and put the box in the bottom of the wardrobe, then she picked up her make up bag. Emma rarely wore make up. She had pale skin and hated the foundation colours that were available. None of them were an exact match. They made her look even more sickly. She just wore black eyeliner and a soft beige lipstick. Emma looked at herself in the mirror, moving her head from one side to the other, checking out each angle. She hadn't been out in over six months. She was dreading it. Why hadn't they decided to go and see a film or just go the pub? But going to see a band as they had on that night — Emma wasn't sure she could hold it together.

When she was ready, she entered Charly's room and sat on the bed, head bowed. 'I'm going out tonight with your dad. I'm going to see a band. I know I've never said this to you before but I'm so sorry. So sorry that I left you that night.' Emma was biting her lip, trying to stop the tears. 'I bet you're thinking how can I go out and leave you again? But you always liked listening to the bands me and your dad love.'

Emma smiled at the memory of Charly pretending she was in the mosh pit at a New Model Army gig. Vagabonds was playing on their dilapidated record player and she'd convinced Robert to let her stand on his shoulders in the garden, while she let her arms dance. She'd seen photographs of the bands fans, The Family, doing just that. Emma was scared she'd slip. At the gigs, they'd be a number of fans holding on to the legs of the brave for support. Here there was just Charly and Robert. She was her daddy's girl. Her daddy's Bat Girl.

'Charly. I will never get over losing you, but I have to live. It's taken me a while to get here. I know that's what you would want. You embraced life. Loved every moment. I know you'd want me and your dad to do the same.' Emma stood up then and picked up one of the Playmobil that sat on top of the chest of drawers. It was a paramedic in a bright green uniform. She popped it in her jacket pocket and left the bedroom.

CHAPTER 101

Robert

Robert reached for his leather jacket. It had the Thunder and Consolation logo painted on the back. He held it to his face and smelled it. It still smelled faintly of dry ice and sweat. He hadn't wore it in six months. He would wear it tonight to the pub and once he got to the gig, hand it over at the cloakroom for a white raffle ticket so it could line up in a row of all the other leather jackets. By the end of the night, he would be shirtless and desperately looking for the raffle ticket, which he'd eventually find crumpled up in the pocket of his black jeans. He'd done this before. Many times.

Tonight, felt different though. He almost wanted to go into that room and apologise to Charly. To ask her permission. Permission to enjoy himself. He put the leather jacket on and stared at himself in the hall mirror. His 'locks were looking tired so he took a tin of oil off the shelf and gently started rubbing it into each separate dread. Encouraging the errant hairs to curl back into the main body. When he'd finished, he stared back at the man he had now become. Each extra line on his forehead a sign of the past six months. He couldn't wear the pink hairband tonight. If he saw any of his old mates, they'd rip him up for it. So, he left the band in the drawer in the hall cupboard.

A short while later, when Emma came downstairs, they left for the pub where they were meeting Nadiah.

CHAPTER 102

Emma

Emma and Robert walked into the Rose and Crown and the pub became silent. Emma almost turned round and went back outside. She held tightly onto Robert's hand. Then Nadiah rushed over and hugged her. By the time Nadiah pulled away, the males in the pub crowd had returned to their pints and their loud conversation. A queue had, also, formed of women all lined up to hug Emma. Some were visibly crying.

I missed you...I wanted to call...I'm so sorry...I'm so glad you are here. One after another the women hugged her. Held on tight as she stared into space behind them feeling uncomfortably numb.

You could tell which of these women had children. They kept a gap between Emma and them. Frightened that it might be catching. That they would be offering their children as the next victim. Their "sorry for your loss" would be louder and more heartfelt, but this was where their closeness ended. Then there was Mandy, obviously pregnant. She was the last in the queue and couldn't look at Emma. So, Emma took the initiative and threw her arms around Mandy. 'It's good to see you,' she said. Mandy physically relaxed in her arms and whispered, 'I'm so sorry, Em.'

Emma held on to her friend. 'I'm fine. Please, don't apologise.' She stepped back and looked down at Mandy's pregnancy bump. 'How many weeks are you? You look blooming.'

Mandy smiled. 'Twenty-six. I don't think I'll be in the mosh pit tonight.'

'I remember with Charly, I saw New Model Army when I was 30 weeks. Robert was like a mother hen and made me stand by the mixing desk all night.' She leant in and whispered into Mandy's ear. 'I just waited until he went into the pit and moved to the front opposite Marshall.'

Mandy laughed. The ice had been broken. Everyone appeared to relax, just like old times. Emma went quiet and watched them. She used to have so much in common with these women, but now she hardly knew them. Forcing them to feel bad on her account wasn't right either. A brave face would be worn and once the band started playing, she hoped that her spirit would be re-energised into her former self, not this empty shell of tormented grief.

CHAPTER 103

Robert

Robert let go of Emma's hand as soon as he saw she was being comforted by her women friends. He spotted Dave at the bar and headed for him. Dave was one of Robert's oldest friends. They'd met at a New Model Army gig just after Robert had left school.

They had since met in this pub every Friday evening for a pint after work. Every Friday evening until that Friday. The night that Charly was murdered. That Friday they had actually broken their pattern. They hadn't met at 3:30pm as they usually did. Returning home to their wives at 5pm. They'd met after 6pm with their wives in tow. Ordered chips to soak up the alcohol. Knew they were in for a long night. The band Roughneck Riot were playing from 8pm and then they planned to go to an after party at the club down the road.

Robert stopped moving towards the bar. His legs were shaking. He remembered that moment. He'd been in the mosh pit facing towards the door with his arms in the air when he saw them. The police, entering the Colly. Searching the crowd for him and Emma.

Coming back to the present, Robert felt himself sinking, he realised that Dave was standing beside him. He gripped his arm and led him to the bar. When he reached it, Robert was able to prop himself up. Dave ordered the drinks. Then gave Robert a crushing hug and whispered, 'Good to see you, mate.'

Robert didn't need to question Dave about why he hadn't rung, texted, come round since Charly died. He didn't question why Dave hadn't come to Charly's funeral. He knew why. Dave had a little girl. The same age as Charly. Robert had wondered over the last six months, if the boot was on the other foot, whether he would have reacted the same way as Dave had. To be fair though, Robert hadn't rung Dave. Hadn't come to the pub on a Friday until now. Tonight's hug and the help to the bar washed all that away. Cleansed it all. They could start again.

'Good to see you too mate,' Robert said.

Dave raised his glass in salute and placed a pint of Robert's favourite beer in front of him. 'Sup that.'

They had a couple of drinks in the Rose and Crown. Robert was relieved they were now just talking about the forthcoming gig and the previous times they had seen Ferocious Dog. Not one of the lads spoke about Charly. Not one even mentioned her name.

CHAPTER 104

Emma

Like a swarm, Emma and her friends walked down Pemberthy Road to the Colly. Nadiah hadn't stopped talking. Emma noticed how much Nadiah fitted in with the crowd. She looked stunning in tight black jeans and knee high black boots. She wore a tight, black vest with a mesh vest in dark khaki over the top, carrying her leather jacket over her arm. Her hair was raven black, crimped and backcombed. Animatedly, she spoke with her hands and eyes. Everyone listened to her every word.

Emma shivered as they turned the corner and could see the front entrance of the Colly. She stopped walking. Nadiah stopped talking. Emma sensed Robert behind her just as he put his hand on her shoulder. She looked up at him and saw the same haunted look on his face. It was decision time. Turn and run; or face some more demons. Emma watched as Nadiah and Dave led everyone away towards the club.

'We can do this,' Robert said.

Emma wasn't sure if he was saying this to himself or her. She could see he was crying. Tears streaming down his face, glistening in the twilight.

She kissed him. Long and hard. Then held his face in her hands. 'Let's go,' she ordered. 'They're all waiting for us.'

Not knowing where her strength came from, all of a sudden, she felt determined. She wanted things to be more normal. Wanted to start enjoying life. Wanted to stop feeling guilty for every small moment of pleasure. For one night, she wanted to be strong for Robert. She took his hand and led him to the club.

There was a long queue of black wearing fans leading up the road and around the corner from the club. All clutching their tickets waiting to be allowed in. Nadiah was standing next to one of the bouncers. She gestured them both over to the front of the queue. Emma was surprised and relieved that the bouncer let them enter ahead of all the others. She knew that if she'd had to wait, there was a chance they'd have given up and gone home.

CHAPTER 105

W

When the wig maker wasn't working or hunting on a Friday night, he came to the Rose and Crown after 6pm. He usually sat with a group of brickies who would come in for one or five after work. He could talk about ridiculous things for a few minutes, but mostly he would feign listening to them while watching out for Robert. He'd been coming here for years.

And there they were, Robert and the delectable, unfaithful Emma being treated like lost sheep returning to the fold. He watched as their good time mates hugged them and slapped them on the back as though this was a cause for celebration. Euphoria should be kept for significant events like murdering a child not for gig going. Anyone can jump up and down, wave their arms in the air and sing.

This pathetic band of travellers with their mohicans, dreads and dyed hair were just society's cast offs, wastrels that needed exterminating. They thought they were being alternative. What a joke! They were arrogant, narcissists thinking they were better than anyone else. That the music they listened to was more accomplished and cleverer than the mainstream. He would teach them.

CHAPTER 106

Emma

As soon as they entered the club, Nadiah led Emma to the front, near the stage. The support act, Louise Distras, was about to start. The crowd parted, like the Red Sea, allowing them access to the barrier which separated the crowd from the stage. This had never happened before. Emma couldn't decide if it was because she was with Nadiah, who was clearly well liked by Stanton's alternative crowd, or whether it was out of pity for her. She hoped it was the former. She didn't want to be the one to be pitied.

Louise Distras' energy consumed them in minutes as she belted out at full volume the first line of The Hand You Hold.

CHAPTER 107

Emma

Louise Distras finished her set and the crowd roared. After years of gig going, Emma knew if she left her space now then she wouldn't be at the front for Ferocious Dog.

Nadiah stood next to her, so Emma took her chance, 'I'm desperate for the toilet, see you back here in a minute.'

'OK. If you fancy going to the bar. I'll have a pint of whatever watered down lager they're selling.' Nadiah smiled.

Emma pushed her way through the crowd and saw Robert by the bar. She walked over to him and planted a kiss on his cheek. 'Be a love and get the drinks in. Get me and Nadiah a lager. I will back in a sec. Just need the loo.'

She didn't give him a chance to reply and headed off to join the queue for the ladies. Emma hated queueing and was relieved when she spotted Rich. At least she'd have someone to chat to until they got to the door. She waved him over. 'I didn't expect to see you here. Why weren't you at the pub?'

'No cash. A friend gave me the ticket for tonight. He couldn't make it so here I am.' Rich grinned. 'Is Robert here then?'

'Yeah. He's at the bar.' Emma blushed. Not sure what to say next.

'You look great, by the way.' Rich nudged her and smiled again.

Remembering how scrawny and unkempt Rich looked on the narrowboat, Emma scrutinised tonight's appearance. His khaki jacket and black t-shirt were clean. His combats and para-boots less so. 'You look…better.'

'Cheers. I'll take that as a compliment.' He moved nearer to her and leant against the wall. Emma stared at his dreadlocks. They were longer and tighter than Robert's. Auburn to Robert's blonde. She was so tempted to run her hands along one but knew how that would look. It was bad enough that he was leaning near her in the queue for the ladies' toilet. If anyone spotted them…

'Listen. I think you're about to go in. Pop by the boat sometime for a coffee,' Rich whispered in her ear. Then moved away back into the crowd.

Emma felt guilty. She wasn't sure why. It wasn't like she'd done anything improper. Just had a chat with an old friend. She hoped she wouldn't blush when she went back to Robert.

By the time she reached Robert at the bar, he'd bought the drinks. Emma kissed him again. On the mouth this time. A soft, brief kiss. Then took the drinks from him and went back into the fray, in search of Nadiah. All thoughts of Rich forgotten. The next couple of hours were for dancing and being normal again. Not a time to think of the past in any of its good or bad guises.

CHAPTER 108

Robert

Robert watched Emma as she swayed and danced. He stood to the side not ready to join the fray in the mosh pit. She looked beautiful tonight. He'd forgotten how much she came alive at gigs. It was what drew him to her in the first place. They had met at a gig. Their first kiss was at a gig. In fact, she'd told him she was pregnant with Charly at a gig. Just before the encore, she'd shouted it in his ear. He'd almost not heard it and didn't quite believe it. Made her repeat it twice. His stomach lurched, remembering the sheer joy of that moment. He wondered if he'd ever feel like that again.

Tonight, Emma had a strength to her that he hadn't seen since Charly's death. A confidence that she had previously lost. She appeared to have escaped the claggy bog of despair even if it was just for a moment.

His phone vibrated in his pocket. It was a text from Patrice. *Where are you? I need to talk to you both?* It simply said. Robert texted back *We are at the Colly, can it wait?*

It took a while before she replied. *It can wait until you get home. Text me then.*

Robert thought of fetching Emma and returning home but decided it was better that they had tonight. He was worried whatever Patrice wanted would ruin their evening. It would be another thing to fight back from. A further pull back into the bog.

CHAPTER 109

DI Chambers

DI Chambers couldn't quite believe it. He had received a call from the Duty Sergeant at 8pm to say that a member of the public had bought in a bag containing a knife stained dark with blood and a razor. The man that dropped it off had said that he'd found it half buried at the back of his house on Draycott Street. He thought it had probably been disturbed by a dog or fox as it was half poking out of the ground.

The razor was plastered with fine, blonde hairs. The canvas bag was distinctive too. It had a shaded paperback on it and the words: Marlowes Bookshop. James recognised it as the bookshop where Emma worked. James checked it, by chance, there was a receipt for books tucked into a corner, but as expected he did not find anything.

The bag and its contents were dispatched immediately to the forensic lab and marked urgent with the case number written in bold.

CHAPTER 110

Emma

Dancing, out of breath. Dancing, singing along. Smiling at Nadiah. The rest of the world melted away. Holding on to the barrier, her now red hair swaying, whipping in time to the music. Hands in the air. Laughing out loud. Nothing mattered for two hours. Nothing.

Then the music stopped. The band left the stage after the final encore. The lights came on and Emma turned away from the stage and searched for Robert. She could see Nadiah, who stood a few feet away from her, engrossed in conversation with a beautiful punk with spiky green hair. Emma could tell by the way these two women were standing close together with hands entwined that this was not the best time to interrupt. She wished Nadiah well. She would phone her sometime tomorrow and thank her for making her come.

She spotted Robert. He was standing by the bar searching all the pockets in his combats. Emma grinned. This was the usual routine. It was like nothing ever really changed. Robert was searching for the cloakroom ticket to reclaim his leather jacket. Emma pushed her hand into the back pocket of her black jeans and pulled out two white tickets. She pushed through the crowd towards Robert. When she was up close, she held out one of the tickets. 'Looking for this,' she said.

It wasn't until they were outside the club that Robert said, 'Patrice texted she wants to meet us.'

Emma was brought immediately back to reality. Robert

hailed a cab and she got in the back. Robert put his arm round her as they sat on the backseat. She felt cold.

CHAPTER 111

Emma

Emma stared at Patrice, who was sitting in her usual armchair. She was angry that Patrice had ruined her evening and why did she always contact Robert, never her? She was the strong one. She was cross with Robert for not telling her straight away that Patrice had contacted him. She scowled in his direction and noticed how worried he looked. He was staring at Patrice. His blond eyebrows scrunched up making the lines on his forehead more prominent.

Patrice broke the silence. 'Early this evening, a member of the public handed in a canvas bag that they had found buried in the back alley behind their house. It contained items which we believe could have been used in a murder or assault. It is very possible that they may be linked to Charly's murder. We've sent them to our forensic labs for further investigation.'

'Could they help trace Charly's murderer?' Robert asked.

'It's too early to say.' Patrice leaned forward in her seat. 'Emma the bag the items were in…it was from the bookshop where you work.'

Emma sat bolt upright. In doing so, she suddenly felt nauseous. She was not sure if it was the shock of the news or the amount she had to drink. She stood up and excused herself. She stumbled up the stairs and pushed open the bathroom door. She just reached the toilet as she started to vomit. She sank to her knees, with one hand on the toilet bowl and the other holding her hair back. As hot liquid, smelling strongly of beer, spewed from her mouth. After a few seconds, she stopped retching and sat back leaning against the bathroom. The coolness of the wall tiles were a relief.

She sat there for a few minutes, then stood up and flushed the toilet. She washed her face and cleaned her teeth. Catching her reflection in the mirror she noticed how ghostly pale she looked, particularly with her pillar-box red hair.

When she went back downstairs, she noticed that Robert had made Patrice tea and there was a mug of black coffee for her on the coffee table. She couldn't face drinking it. She sat down on the sofa. Robert asked if she was ok. No doubt the two of them had heard her vomiting. She said she was fine. Then Patrice said, 'We will need to look at the bookshop records. Can we have the owner's mobile number then we can ring him and get him to open up for us tomorrow?'

Emma went to get her jacket from where she had left it thrown over the wooden banisters in the hall. Her phone was in the pocket. She got it out and saw that Nadiah had texted her: Had *a fab night. In more ways than one :-} speak tomorrow. Xx* It all seemed such a long time ago. She searched her contacts for her bosses number and forwarded it to Patrice, she wanted her to leave now. She felt drained.

CHAPTER 112

w

    The Wig Maker woke early. Frustrated that the hair he had left was too fine to weave. He gathered it into a pile on his desk. Rolled it out. Tried to hook it, ready to weave. But it was useless. He stabbed the desk with the hook and caught the edge of his other hand. It didn't bleed at first. Then it flowed. He pulled his hand up away from the table. Worried the blood would stain the wig. Ruin it.

    He went downstairs to kitchen. Put his hand under the tap. Watched the blood flow down the sink. It reminded him of the times he had cut himself. The relief swirling. Short-lived. Lasting as long as the blood gurgled down the plug hole.

    The relief had been the same with the girls and just as short-lived. Murder did nothing for him. It was just a necessary act.

CHAPTER 115

Emma

It was 7am on a warm Sunday morning. Emma stood outside the bookshop waiting for the police to arrive. She shivered despite the warmth. Her mum would have said that "someone had just stepped on to her grave". That was exactly how she felt. Her daughter's killer knew where she worked. All this time she had blamed Robert and maybe it was her fault. Maybe she was the reason that the killer had chosen Charly. She pulled her PVC jacket closer around her and moved further into the doorway.

Five minutes later, DI Chambers and a PC, who introduced herself as Sara Mason, arrived at the bookshop. Emma opened up the bookshop for them. Her boss had told her to use the back-office computer and had given her all the necessary passwords. This was unlike him, but he was away playing golf in Wales and Emma guessed that he didn't want to have to come back to Stanton. He, also, wouldn't want the Sunday trade spoiled by the presence of the two police officers.

Emma opened up the sales records. She wasn't sure what the officers would be looking for, so she carefully explained all aspects of the search facility. Then she left them to their search and went to the tiny kitchen area to make them coffee.

CHAPTER 114

DI Chambers

'What shall we search for, first?' Sara asked her boss.

'Let's start with the employee list from Asda. We could check it against card payments,' DI Chambers replied.

Sara took the list out of the manila folder that she had brought with her. She typed in each name. There was a list of romance titles for one of the women cashiers. A list of crime novels for the Deputy Manager. These were mostly Mark Billinghams and Val McDermids. Both authors Sara, also, loved, though she wasn't going to admit that to her boss.

'Is there a print facility?' Sara asked Emma.

'Sorry, yes there is. If you go to the print icon in the top left had corner it will print to the shop printer in the main part of the bookshop,' replied Emma.

Sara printed the lists of books she had found. Emma went to fetch the paper copies from the printer.

DI Chambers said to Sara, 'Run a check for books about hair or wig making.'

Sara didn't question why he was asking this. She ran the check. Only one match came back: Costume Design and Wig Making by Susan Bradshaw. There was an order generated with a name and address. It was for Mike Deyton and the address sounded familiar. The book was collected two weeks later and paid for in cash. Sara showed James what she had found, and he rang one of the MIT team to check that the address matched Mike Deyton's. He confirmed that it did.

'I thought that we had ruled Mike Deyton out, sir,' Sara

said.

'He was working the night of Samantha's murder. We checked, and he had arrived at the venue at 6pm to set up. He didn't leave until 2 in the morning.'

'So, someone used his identity.'

Emma came back at that moment. 'You've found something?' she asked.

Sara hesitated. She wasn't sure how much she could say. It was such an odd search. How would it be explained to Emma without having to tell her about her daughter's hair removal.

James spoke, 'A Mike Deyton had his car stolen on the day of Samantha's murder. We've checked, and a book was ordered and bought by him, or someone using his name, called Costume Design and Wig Making. Do you remember the sale by any chance?'

Sara noticed that Emma had gone unusually pale at the mention of the book.

'Yes, it was such an odd request, I remember it well,' Emma muttered.

'Emma, this is important. Can you describe the person who bought the book?' Sara asked.

'Yes. He was about my age. He had dark hair which was parted in the middle. It looked odd. He was very muscular. He looked like a bodybuilder, which was why I thought it was an odd choice of book,' Emma replied.

'Could he have been wearing a wig?' James asked.

Emma looked confused. 'Possibly,' she said.

Sara and James left with print outs of the search results. They arranged for Emma to come to the station the next day to look at some photographs. They had a photograph of Mike Deyton that he had agreed to have taken in the hope of eliminating himself from enquiries. They could, also, make an e-fit of the man that Emma had served as a customer.

CHAPTER 115

Emma

Emma arrived at the police station at 8am. She sat and waited for DI Chambers to call her into the interview room. She recalled how Robert had quizzed her for hours the night before. *Who was this Mike Deyton? Did the police suspect him? What had costume design got to do with it?* She was waiting for the accusations, but they never came. *If he was stalking you, then it is your fault.* That was what Emma now thought. All night she had tossed and turned. Seeing pictures of the bodybuilder in her head. His physique got larger and larger through the night. His face shape and features constantly changing, until she wasn't sure what was real and what was imagined. The only constant was the middle parting in his hair and DI Chambers had suggested that this was a wig.

Then a PC came and took her to Interview Room 3. DI Chambers was waiting for her. He had a tablet open showing a number of photographs. For some reason Emma had been expecting a table full of photographs, which she would be expected to inspect; or maybe even a police lineup with the suspect in, looking sheepish. But of course, this was the digital age, and everything was now computer based.

'I want you to look at these photographs,' he said slowly, 'let me know if anyone looks familiar to you. Look at each of them a couple of times first. Don't worry if you do not see him or are unsure.'

Emma looked at each photograph in turn. None of them looked familiar. Their head shape and features were completely different to the man she had served. She was sure of it. 'I don't recognise any of them,' she said.

'Are you sure?' James asked.

'Yes, certain,' Emma responded.

The man, Emma assumed was a Police Constable, then sat down next to Emma.

'My name is Peter Johnson, I'm a forensic artist.' He said.

Emma expected him to use a tablet like the one held by DI chambers, but instead he reached into the bag he had with him and got out a box of pencils and a sketch pad. They worked solidly for an hour until Emma was happy with the sketch. The artist had painstakingly drawn the lightest of lines and rubbed out the unnecessary ones until the outline was complete. He then shaded the drawing until it looked just like the man she had served in the bookshop. Emma could now see know why DI Chambers had asked if his hair was a wig. The hair looked wholly unrealistic in this form.

Before the forensic artist left, DI Chambers asked him to draw other versions with completely different hairstyles. Emma could barely look at each sketch in case it looked familiar to her. The thought that this man had been stalking her, terrified her. She didn't recognise any of them though. But this didn't make her relax. Even hours after leaving the police station she felt apprehensive and anxious.

CHAPTER 116

Robert

Robert arrived home at a little after 6pm. Emma was in the kitchen peeling vegetables. She smiled when he walked past. He went straight to the fridge and helped himself to a cold beer.

'It's been one of those days,' he said as he took a large gulp of beer.

He wondered what was up. Emma didn't react at all. She didn't tut or sigh or ask for her own beer. Instead she continued to peel the vegetables.

'Did you want one?' he eventually asked.

Emma shook her head. Then he noticed she was crying. Crying without sound. A steady stream of tears flowing down her face and dripping off her chin. Robert grabbed some kitchen roll and passed it to her. She dabbed her face and eyes.

'Bad day too?' Robert asked. Then he remembered that Emma had been to the police station. He'd been so caught up in scaffold planks and angry builders that he'd forgotten that Emma had gone to identify the guy who she had served in the bookshop.

'I wasn't much help,' Emma finally said.

'How do you know?'

'The photo they showed me first definitely wasn't him. Then some forensics guy got me to describe him and he sketched what I said. By the end it was pretty close to the guy I remembered, but now the more I think, the more I'm not sure. Maybe the guy I described doesn't look like him at all?'

'Why don't we go back to Asda tomorrow. Now you know you've probably seen him, you might be able to spot him in the supermarket.'

Emma dropped the knife she was holding. It clattered on the draining board and fell into the sink with a splash.

'It's all a game to you. Do you really think I want to go hunting for him!' Emma screamed.

'You did before,' muttered Robert. He was going to give her a hug but thought better of it. It was usually better to let Emma burn herself out. Robert hated confrontation.

Emma left the rest of the vegetables unpeeled and went upstairs. He heard a door slam. He guessed it was Charly's room Emma had entered. He took another long slug of beer and finished preparing the dinner. Doubtful that Emma would join him but hoping that she would.

CHAPTER 117

Robert

Robert woke early and reached over to Emma's side of the bed hoping for an early morning cuddle. But she wasn't there. She must have slept all night in Charly's bed. He went downstairs and made himself breakfast. Quickly showered and shaved and left for work.

It was raining. Fine, drizzly rain that soaked through his leathers. By the time he reached work, he was wet and miserable. He hadn't spoken to Emma. He didn't plan to. Not quite yet.

Mariam was switching on the kettle when he entered the office.

'Cuppa?' she asked.

'No time,' Jack said as he walked through the door taking off his raincoat and hanging it up.

Robert just shrugged, and Mariam raised her eyebrows.

'I want you leading the team today. There's a list of jobs for you. It will be full on. I hope you've brought a packed lunch,' Jack didn't wait for any protest. He didn't expect any.

Robert hadn't brought any lunch. He was planning on riding home at lunchtime and maybe catching Emma before she went to work. Now he would have to stop off at Greggs or Asda before doing the first job. The lads arrived a few minutes later and they left the yard.

It was the last job of the day. A tricky one. Some of the planks they had left were too short. Robert was hungry and tired. Upset that he hadn't seen or heard from Emma. She wasn't picking up his texts or answering her phone. He just wanted to get this job finished and go home.

Martin, the apprentice, shouted from the top planks, 'Bring me up some bolts. I've run out.'

Robert shimmied up the scaffold. Rushing with the bag of bolts. More concerned about speed than safety. He reached the top boards. The guardrails were not yet in place. He was supposed to attach himself to the mid rail using a safety line, but he didn't bother.

Robert handed Martin the bag of bolts. For the first time in his life, he felt dizzy. The boards felt like they were moving under his feet. He stepped to the side in the hope of gaining balance but there was no guardrail to support him. So he fell. Twenty feet.

CHAPTER 118

Emma

Emma arrived at work early. She had left the house after she heard Robert leave, not wanting to talk to him. Walking to work always cleared her head. She thought about Rich. Maybe she should go to his boat. For a talk nothing more. But did Rich have other motives?

When they were younger, in their late teens, they were inseparable. Both attended the school in the next town. Emma because she had been bullied in her first year at Parks Mead. She stood out. Enjoyed different music to the rest of her class. Liked to read on her own instead of hanging around in a crowd. Her mum had decided better to move to another school rather than tackle the issue. Emma had been bullied there too but she decided not to tell her mum as there was nowhere else for her to go. Besides, she got on really well with her new English teacher. She was always suggesting new books for Emma to devour.

Rich had been expelled from Parks Mead for calling his form tutor a wanker and damaging school property. The way Rich told the story, he was the hero. His form teacher had made some inappropriate remarks to some of the female students. While the rest of his class seemed to have decided that it was better to put up with it than complain, Rich had decided that it was better to tackle it head on. He'd basically thrown a chair at the teacher when he told him he should lighten up.

So, there they both were in their second year at a Secondary School in a different town to where they lived. Two misfits. They spent the rest of their time trying to shock students and teachers alike. Going for the most outlandish hair colours and adapting their uniform as much as they could get away with.

They saw each other both in and out of school. Went shopping together on a Saturday. Bought vinyl from the guy selling alternative music on the market. Spent the afternoon in Emma's house discussing and listening to what they had bought. Dyed each other's hair. Drunk cider on the swings in the local park. Told each other their wildest dreams. Plotted going to festivals they couldn't afford.

They had only kissed once. They were at the park, lying on their backs watching the clouds and talking about The Cure and Rich had rolled over, stroked Emma's chin and leant in for a kiss. It was nice, but it left them both feeling embarrassed and awkward for the rest of the day. Neither mentioned it again. In fact, Emma only remembered it occasionally and wondered what would have happened if they'd gone any further. She could still remember how soft Rich's lips were and how he tasted of spearmint.

By the time she arrived at work, all thoughts of Rich had dissipated. There was a pile of new stock that needed stacking on shelves. It was a laborious and often boring job. The only skill it required was knowing the order of the alphabet. Emma would occasionally spot a book that really interested her and would often spend a few moments reading the blurb and the first chapter while her boss wasn't looking.

She was absorbed again in the latest psychological thriller when she subconsciously felt a set of eyes bearing into her. She put the book on the shelf and reached for the next one. As she went to shelve it she noticed that there was a piece of paper poking out of the top. Occasionally, the sale notice was left in. Emma sighed and pulled it out.

It took her a moment to work out what it said. It looked like someone had cut letters out of a newspaper and glued them on. The letter began: *Dear Emma*. It was for her. She nearly dropped it in shock. She started to read it again.

Dear Emma,

I know your little secret but I'm guessing Robert doesn't. Having an affair with a crusty on a boat. Tut tut.

It's no wonder you no longer have a daughter. Neither of you deserved her.

It wasn't signed.

Emma's hands shook. Was he still here watching her? She searched around the shop in a panic.

One of the other assistants, Marc spotted her, 'Emma, what's up. You look like you've seen a ghost?'

She came to her senses then. Decided that she couldn't show anyone the letter as they might believe that she really was seeing Rich. And she wasn't. Nothing was happening between them.

She calmed down, walked to the staff room and stuffed the letter in her bag.

CHAPTER 119

Emma

Emma received a call from Jack as she was about to leave work. She asked him to repeat what he was saying three times before she would believe him. Jack didn't seem to know what condition Robert was in, only that he'd fallen twenty feet from a scaffold and had been taken to Stanton University Hospital. Emma waited outside the bookshop for Jack to pick her up.

She stood rigidly with her phone in her hand, dreading another call. Convinced Robert was dead. In her head, she was back at her mum's waiting for news of her missing daughter. In reality, she was oblivious to the people walking past in the street. Even those that were stumbling into her. She was just waiting for the police to arrive to tell her what she already knew that her daughter was dead. She jumped, as the phone buzzed. It was a text from Jack, he was parked up on the other side of the bookshop. Emma ran to his car.

On the way to the hospital, Jack kept talking. He was saying how it wasn't his fault. Robert had gone to attach himself to the mid pole and slipped. One of the apprentices had tried to catch him but it all happened so fast. A complete accident. He was sure Robert would be okay. He was made of strong stuff. Emma heard the words, but they meant nothing. She was alone now. She could sense it. Just as she sensed it when Charly died. She didn't need Patrice to tell her they had found a body. She knew. And now she knew that Robert was dead.

They arrived at the hospital ten minutes later, Jack came round to her side of the car and helped her out like she was an invalid. There was a huge queue at A and E reception. Jack led Emma to a chair. 'I will go and get someone,' he said.

Emma didn't reply. She just looked around her. Not really seeing anything. Numb.

Jack came back minutes later with a nurse. 'I can take you to Robert,' the nurse said,

'I don't want to see him,' Emma said. 'I can't see him like that. I couldn't see Charly. I can't see Robert. I just can't.'

'Emma,' Jack said. 'Robert's not dead. He's not good, but he's not dead. Come on lets go and see him.'

He helped Emma up and led her to the trauma unit to the left of Reception. The nurse held the door open. Emma could barely see Robert. He was surrounded by doctors and nurses. All had a specific job to do. All busy taking blood, monitoring his heart rate and talking in what sounded to Emma like a foreign language. All she wanted to do was hold his hand…arm…stroke his face…anything. Eventually the mass of bodies parted, and she could see that Robert was awake. Clearly in pain, but awake. He wore a neck brace so was staring at the ceiling. Emma moved to the top of the bed where he could see her. He smiled at her. A forced smile, almost a grimace, but a smile nonetheless.

'He's very lucky,' one of the doctors said. 'He's broken a few ribs and we are waiting to take him for a head scan, so we won't know the full extent of his injuries yet, but he's lucky not to have more serious injuries.'

'I bounced off one of the lower boards. Don't ask me how,' Robert muttered.

Emma kissed his forehead. It was warm and sticky.

The rest of the evening went in a blur. Robert had a concussion and one of his ribs had nicked a lung. He had to have a chest drain fitted but he was alive. That was all that mattered. Emma went home at 3am when Robert was taken onto a ward. Jack drove her home in silence. Emma was glad as she was too tired and drained to talk.

CHAPTER 120

Emma

Emma woke with a start the next morning. Disorientated she reached for Robert, before remembering he was in hospital. She had no work today and the hospital had told her that visiting wasn't until 2pm for relatives. She could go and buy Robert new toiletries and nightclothes. He would appreciate that.

Her bag was hanging up in the hall. Emma wondered if she had enough cash to get the bus straight from Asda to the hospital. She searched around in the bottom of her bag for her purse. Not finding it, she started to pull things out. A copy of Val McDermid's The Vanishing Point came out first, followed by a moleskin notebook — Robert had bought her this for her birthday to record her musings — and then out came a white envelope.

Emma had forgotten the note that she'd found in the shop. After Robert's fall, all memory of it had been erased, she had been more concerned about the plight of her surviving love, to care about the triviality of blackmail.

She put her bag down, sat on the bottom stair and opened the note again. What would Robert do if he read the note? Would he believe that her meeting Rich was completely innocent. When she started seeing Robert, Rich gallantly slipped into the background. He would rarely call Emma, only chat to her when they were coincidently in the same place. Even then the conversation was stilted. They didn't laugh together, hug or share secrets like they used to. It had made Emma feel sad and lonely. But as her relationship blossomed with Robert, she forgot about her friendship with Rich. He became peripheral. When he left in his narrowboat for Bristol, Emma simply waved him goodbye and wished him luck. He must have been sad about this, thinking back. Now, he would know what to do. Whether she should simply come clean or brush it all under the carpet. She would visit him soon.

An hour later Emma was trawling the shelves at Asda trying to find some nightclothes and slippers that wouldn't make Robert look like a pensioner. She looked up from a particularly hideous looking pair of pyjama bottoms and saw Nadiah waving at her from the back of the shop.

'How's Robert?' Nadiah said as soon as Emma reached her.

'How do you know what happened?' Emma said, briefly forgetting what small-town England was like.

'One of the nurses comes in here at the end of the night shift, she told me.' Nadiah explained. 'Will he be in long?'

'No idea. I hope not, I hate being in the house on my own.'

'Why don't I come round and keep you company later. I can bring some drink if you like and a pizza. What time does evening visiting end?'

'About 8. I should be home by 8:30 at a push.'

'I can get my cousin Mo to pick you up if you want? He lives round the corner from the hospital.'

'No, it's fine. Thanks.' Emma felt relieved that she wouldn't have to spend the whole evening alone.

When she carried on searching for pyjamas, she started to feel uneasy. The hairs stood up on the back of her neck. She was glad when she had found something mildly suitable, had paid and left the shop.

CHAPTER 121

W

The wig maker hadn't expected to see Emma today. This was a bonus. He hoped she'd read his note. Maybe it was in her bag…festering.

He had, also, heard that Robert had fallen from a scaffold. It was a shame the damage hadn't been fatal. Mind you if Robert died, he wouldn't feel the pain of what was going to happen in the coming days. The task needed completing as soon as possible. The opportunity may never be as good. He would sneak out of work early and fetch his new set of tools from their hiding place under the sink.

CHAPTER 122

Nicole

It was after 6pm on a Friday. Nicole was studying at the dining room table. Her books were strewn everywhere. The girls were in their pyjamas watching cartoons on the television. Nicole had an essay to write comparing the work of the Bronte sisters. Over the last few days, she had re-read all of their works, but was having trouble with the word length. She could write for months on the subject. Instead of being in Stanton, she imagined herself walking the Yorkshire Moors wearing a bustled crinoline dress and bonnet. Searching for her tall, dark lover. Her pleading voice being carried by the wind.

She glanced up at the window and saw a shadow moving along the back wall. She stood up with a start and moved towards the window. Standing by the side of it at this angle she could see out and anyone in the yard could not see in. There was someone in the yard. Dressed in dark clothes with their hood pulled up. Carrying a black bag. They seemed to be doing something to the back-door lock.

'We need to leave, now,' Nicole whispered, as she moved towards the sofa.

She picked up Rosie and held her tightly, scared she would start crying. Holly got up immediately, hearing the urgency in her mother's voice. The cartoon instantly forgotten. They moved quickly towards the front door. Nicole decided their best bet would be to go to Pete and Sean's two doors down. Pete was a firefighter. He would scare anyone off. She opened the door and they all ran. As soon as she reached the neighbour's house, she banged on the door. Sean answered. He was only wearing a towel. His black hair still damp from the shower.

'What the hells the matter. Pete's just come off his shift. He's having a nap,' Sean said.

'There's someone breaking into my house,' Nicole said. Rosie was crying now. Holly was holding on to Nicole's legs. Both sensing their mother's fear.

Pete came to the door. His brown curly hair flattened by sleep.

'Out the back?' he said, having plainly heard Nicole.

They let Nicole into their house. Sean stayed with them in the front room Pete raced out of the back door.

Ten minutes later Pete came back into the house, puffing. 'I couldn't see anyone. I ran down the back of our houses and up to the main road too. I've checked your back door lock - it looks fine.'

'You should call the police,' Sean pleaded.

'I'd rather just get my stuff and go to my mums for the night. If I call the police I'd have to stay at the house or here and they will probably be hours,' Nicole said.

She looked around the couple's room. Fortunately, the girls were tired and were cuddled up next to her on the sofa. If she stayed here to wait for the police, they would trash the place in five minutes. Everything was neatly placed and colour coordinated. The exact opposite of her house.

'Pete, do you mind coming with me to get some things then we can get the bus to my mum's she only lives in Stockford Road?' Nicole asked.

'Don't be daft the girls can stay with me, while you get your stuff then Pete will drive you all to Stockford Road. It can't be more than five minutes' drive. Won't you Pete?' Simon enthused.

Pete looked far from impressed by this idea. 'Yeah of course I will,' he said.

Nicole was concerned that she was taking advantage of their neighbourliness but Simon seemed more than happy to babysit and the girls were comfortable with him. Besides it would just be for a short time. Pete seemed less enthusiastic but clearly wanted to please Simon by going along with the plan.

Ten minutes later and the girls were curled up on the backseat of Pete's car. Nicole held a carrier bag filled with their clothes and toothbrushes, plus a spare pair of knickers for herself.

'I'm sorry I don't have car seats. I hope I don't get you into trouble.' She said to Pete, who seemed mildly annoyed that he'd been inconvenienced.

'As long as they keep their heads down no one will notice. You will go to the police won't you. I mean if you saw someone breaking in. You don't want to spend the next few weeks worried all the time.'

Nicole took this to mean that he thought she was being paranoid. There was no one breaking in and please don't bother me and Sean again. She just said, 'I will.'

Fortunately, they were just about to enter Stockford Road so Nicole directed Pete to the fifth house down with the caravan on the drive. The girls sat up.

Nicole said a mumbled, 'Thanks' and got out of the car with the girls as fast as she could.

CHAPTER 123

Emma

Emma got back from the hospital at 9pm. Robert was spaced out on painkillers and hadn't said much. His parents had arrived and pretty much dominated the time spent with Robert. They wanted to know exactly what happened. Robert seemed to think he'd just slipped but Emma told them what Jack said — that he was moving between poles and hadn't managed to attach the carabiner yet.

Robert's mum said that she thought he might be able to claim against Jack. Robert went mad at this. Jack had been so good since Charly died. Emma was glad when the bell rang and rushed out so she could get the bus home and wouldn't need to talk anymore to Robert's parents. Then she felt guilty for not saying a proper goodbye to Robert.

Nadiah arrived at 9:30pm. She'd bought a bottle of vodka and a vegetable pizza. At least she'd remembered that she was a vegetarian. They ate quickly and drank a couple of vodka and cokes each.

'I can do your hair for you if you like. I've brought some styling wax with me.' Nadiah suggested.

'So, Robert is in hospital and I'm having my hair done?' Emma said.

'He will appreciate it too when you see him tomorrow. Go and get it washed and then I will blow dry it for you.'

Emma went to the bathroom, showered and washed her hair. The bath she was standing in was splattered with red dye. She'd only dyed her hair a few nights ago and it was still leaking from her hair when it was soaped.

She got out of the bath and dried herself with one of her older towels and put on her red toweling dressing gown, tying it tightly with its belt.

When she went downstairs Nadiah had put on some old Sisters of Mercy and Black Planet was belting out from the speakers. They still owned a turntable and amp. Emma kept suggesting they replaced it with a digital system, but Robert wouldn't hear of it.

Emma sat down on one of the dining room chairs and Nadiah started to dry her hair. It didn't take long but it gave Emma the chance to properly relax. She liked the touch of Nadiah's hands as she held her hair closer to the dryer, not bothering with a comb or brush. When Nadiah had finished drying Emma's hair, she rubbed styling wax onto her hands and started pulling clumps of hair into a spiky punk style,

'Did you enjoy the gig the other night?' Nadiah asked.

The gig seemed so long ago. 'Yes,' Emma answered. 'I noticed you seemed to too.'

Nadiah laughed, 'Deana is an old friend. Well…more than a friend. I don't think I've ever told you I am bi and let's face it the male talent…lots of middle aged sweaty men…no thank you.'

'No one at work take your fancy?'

'Asda? Are you having a laugh? The talent there is dire.'

This brought Emma back to reality. 'Did that guy come back to work?'

'Guy? Oh, you mean Josh. No, he never did. Good riddance I say. He used to give me the creeps. Never spoke to me or any of the other staff, yet he used to follow blonde women around the shop.'

Emma shivered. Nadiah noticed and said, 'Blonde women not girls.'

'I tell you what…,' Nadiah continued, 'There are some right weirdos that work at my place.'

Emma listened as Nadiah described each staff member in

turn. The checkout women with errant husbands and romantic daydreams. The fishmonger who kept snakes and used to have dead mice in his locker. The trolley collector who never takes his cap off even indoors. 'I've never seen his hair and he's always hanging about inside the shop. The state of the trolleys too…I'm surprised he's never had the sack.'

Emma sat bolt upright. 'Do you think it's him?' she said,

'Him what?' asked Nadiah.

'The killer. It could be him. He's always in the shop… never takes his cap off.'

'Don't say that. He lives two streets down from me. Now you're giving me the creeps.'

'I want to see his house. Can we go there in the morning?'

'Why on earth would you want to see his house?'

'Well if we go early enough, he's not likely to be wearing his cap is he, I mean he won't wear it in bed.'

'Okay, but you will have to knock his door. He knows me. And it can't be tomorrow. I'm working from 6. It will have to be Tuesday.'

He knows me too, thought Emma. Not sure why she'd even suggested this mad idea but knowing that she had to go through with it. If she saw his whole face she would know. She would know it was him and then she could go to the police.

CHAPTER 124

Nicole

Nicole and the girls returned to their house early Monday morning. Nicole couldn't bear being around her mother and step dad much longer. They were always shouting and screaming at each other. Nicole couldn't have her girls listening to that. She'd had to put up with it for the last two years before leaving home. Out of necessity, she'd left at sixteen and gone to work at a greengrocers that had a small bedsit above. Holly was born six months after she'd got her job. Having a child meant that she could move into a housing association flat. As soon as she could, she went back to college and got her A levels. She hadn't minded claiming benefits and studying. They even had a free creche attached for *social work referrals.* She hated that label, but she was determined to make something of her life. To make Holly proud. She didn't care what her mum thought.

She was so disappointed with herself when she caught for Rosie. It was only her second year of university and she'd had a fling with the union president. Neither of them could believe it when she found out she was pregnant. He had even run home to his parents to decide what *he* wanted. Nicole knew what she wanted *a sister for Holly.* She knew she could cope with children and studying as she was already doing it.

She always coped on her own so returning to her house was the only option. Besides she had an essay to finish. She turned the key in the lock and ushered Holly in, holding Rosie and the carrier bag in one arm. Holly rushed off as soon as she got in. Nicole assumed she'd gone to her room. The bus journey had been a nightmare. Without the buggy, Nicole had to hold Rosie the whole way. She had been snuffly and fussy, crying and moaning. Nicole was relieved that she was now asleep and had put her down to sleep on the sofa. She then made herself a cup of tea and sat at the table; reading back through her essay checking where she was up to. All she wanted was half an hour's peace. The trauma of Friday evening forgotten in the moment.

Nicole was just finishing a section on Wuthering Heights when she heard a piercing scream. Not sure where it came from, she stood up in panic. Where was Holly? She shouted he name upstairs. Nothing. She ran to the back door which was wide open. Rushing outside into the yard Nicole saw that the back gate was open too. 'No,' she moaned.

She ran out of the yard into the back entry and there was a man with his hand clasped around Holly's mouth dragging her backwards to a waiting car. Nicole sprinted towards him and started screaming and hitting him across his arm and body. Persistently hitting him and screaming. Holly looked terrified but somehow managed to open her mouth and sink her teeth into the man's hand. He let go for a split second. He must have seen that to fight this crazy woman as he sped off towards a blue car.

As soon as Nicole got back into the house, she rang the police. They arrived within fifteen minutes. Holly was inconsolable, feeding off her mother's tension. This bled on to Rosie, who was now awake and screaming. The police officer introduced himself as DS Khapor. He clearly was having trouble understanding what Nicole was saying. She was shaking, the girls still crying. He offered to have one of the PCs look after them, but they wouldn't be removed from her. In the end, after getting brief descriptions of the car and abductor, DS Khapor left Nicole with a PC.

'I will get a member of Family Liaison to sit with you and there will be a couple of officers around the house for the next few hours at least,' DS Khapor told Nicole, then he left.

Nicole sat with the PC and drank a constant supply of tea, holding tightly onto her two girls.

CHAPTER 125

W

 The wig maker returned to his home. He was sweating and shaking as he unlocked his front door. He had made a huge mistake. He couldn't believe his luck when he returned to the girl's house to find her playing in the yard. He knew if he was quick he could grab a child in daylight, as he had with the last one. She'd been too busy feeding those rabbits when he'd come up behind her and hit her over the head. But this time the girl had heard him enter the yard and screamed. He'd dropped the brick he was holding and stupidly, instead of just running back to the car, he had tried to stop her by clamping her mouth shut and pulling her away.

 He sat down on the settee trying to calm his breathing, so he could think straight. He'd dumped the car on a piece of wasteland about two miles away. It was stolen, and he'd set fire to it. Hopefully that was enough. He had been wearing a black hoodie and the bottom half of his face was covered by a neck warmer, like motorcyclists wore. She wouldn't have seen his whole face. He pinched the back of his hand hard. He needed to calm down. Nothing bad was going to happen. He could blend back into the shadows.

CHAPTER 126

Emma

Approaching the narrowboat, Emma wondered if her child's killer was following her today. If he had a letter ready for Robert. "Your wife is having an affair with a New Age traveller while you are laid up in hospital." She shivered and boarded the boat.

She tapped on the door and Rich opened it almost immediately. He must have seen her coming up the towpath. He hugged her to him. His chin resting on her shoulder. For a moment, she didn't want to let him go. He smelled of coconut oil and his dreads tickled like Robert's.

Eventually, she pulled away.

Rich asked, 'Can I get you a coffee or a tea or something?'

'A tea would be nice.' Emma sat on the sofa and stared across the water at the opposite towpath. *Maybe they should shut the curtains.*

Emma shivered again.

Rich put a tray of tea and a small plate of biscuits on the table and sat down next to her.

Emma said, 'Robert's in hospital.'

'What?' Worry lines formed on Rich's forehead and he took Emma's hand in his. 'What the hell happened?'

Emma took her hand away. Concerned how it might look.

'He fell from a scaffold. About twenty feet.'

Rich looked even more worried.

Emma continued. 'He's not too bad…considering.'

'Bloody hell. That's awful, Moon…I mean Em.' Rich

looked at the floor.

Emma didn't know how to tell him about the letter. It was burning a hole in the bottom of her bag. She could just show it to him. Let him read it. Let him make up his mind where it came from. In her heart, Emma believed it was from her daughter's killer. Why she felt this, she wasn't sure. There was no major evidence that it was. Just a gnawing feeling, deep in her gut. It had kept her awake all night. Thinking, that monster who killed her daughter was now taunting and threatening her. What made it worse was the one person she thought she could always turn to, she couldn't even speak to about this. But Rich might be able to help.

'I've had a letter. Someone left it in the shop addressed to me. They'd hidden it in a book.' Emma got the envelope out of her bag and showed the letter to Rich.

'Blimey, it's like a spy novel. How weird.' Rich smiled. 'Don't let it get to you. It's all rubbish.'

Emma chewed her lip. 'I can't bear the thought of Robert reading it.'

'Why Moon? It's not like we've ever done anything.'

'I know that and you know that. But since Charly died, things haven't been easy. We're not as close as we were. I've told him I've met you on the boat, but this might put major doubts in his head.'

Rich sighed and again took hold of Emma's hand. 'I guess that's normal, but I'm sure he still trusts you. All you've got to do is tell him the truth.'

Emma was still biting her lip. 'But what if he doesn't believe me!'

Rich put his arm around Emma and hugged her. 'I'm more concerned about who's written the letter. Someone has either managed to be on the tow path just at the same time as you or...' He hugged Emma a little tighter. 'Or they are following you.'

'They're stalking me, Rich.' Emma leant into Rich's chest. 'Do you think…? No, I can't think this. It can't be Charly's killer can it?'

'I think you need to go to the police. If you need me to, I can come. I'll tell them there's nothing going on between us.'

Emma started to cry. She pushed her face into Rich's jumper, shoulders heaving.

Rich stroked her hair. 'Moon, you can stay here if you want while Robert is in hospital. You can take the bed and I'll take the sofa.'

Emma sat bolt upright like a frightened rabbit. Brought to her senses by the suggestion. 'Then it will be true won't it!'

Rich sat back, giving Emma space. 'What will be true?'

'That I'm having an affair with a crusty on a boat.' She got up and searched round for her bag.

When she'd found it. She hugged it to her.

'We've not kissed or anything...' Rich blushed.

'But you've thought about it.'

'And you haven't?'

'No' Emma practically ran off the boat. She slipped on the deck and grabbed the side of the boat, lurching her back into sensibleness.

They hadn't had an affair. They hadn't come close. But she was running away because that was what she feared. If Rich attempted to kiss her, that she wouldn't stop him. She sat down on one of the cushions arranged around the front outdoor seating. Rich hadn't followed her. He was probably upset at being accused, because what she really meant was that she had thought about it. Of course, this was all ridiculous. She'd told Robert that she'd met Rich on the boat. She hadn't lied or kept it a secret. So why couldn't she show him the letter?

She felt something warm and soft rubbing her leg. It was Moonbeam. The dog must have been asleep under the seat. Moonbeam rested his head on her lap and Emma stroked it. *Rich still called her Moon. That was the problem. Robert called her Emma and Rich called her Moon.*

CHAPTER 127

DI Chambers

DI Chambers was at work early. He had spoken to DS Khapor about the possible abduction of another child Holly Stretton the previous evening. He was preparing a report for the case review when PC Sara Mason tapped on his door. She was holding a file, she walked over to his desk and held it out to him. 'This is the forensic report on the three cars,' she said.

James took it off her and thanked her. He opened the file. The top two reports were for Josh Cummins' cars. There was nothing discovered in either which was what James had expected. He was even more convinced of Josh's innocence. The third report was for Mike Deyton's car. There were no fingerprints anywhere on the car except for Mike Deyton's. There was evidence that the car had been steam cleaned inside and power washed. Even the wheel arches were immaculate. James would get one of the officers to check with Mike that he hadn't recently cleaned it. He had been using his van more recently and he'd previously told the team that he hadn't used his cars in the days before it was impounded.

There was only one significant piece of evidence. A piece of plastic with a minute sample of blood on it had been found attached to the spare wheel rim. The forensic team had checked. It was Samantha's blood.

The killer had made two clear mistakes. The attempted abduction and the plastic left in the car. James suspected that he'd wrapped Samantha's body in plastic. It was a particularly thick variety like garden rubbish bags. The plastic must then have caught on the wheel rim as he tried to force the body into the car.

James went into the incident room and marked the position of Mike Deyton's house on the map and then the position of Nicole's home. They were in walking distance of each other. In fact, all of the important locations were within a two mile zone. James had never doubted that the killer was living in Stanton. Living in Stanton and possibly working at Asda. Stalking and killing blonde, six-year-old girls. He was someone's neighbour, someone's son and maybe someone's partner or husband. In his gut, James doubted he was married. He doubted he had a partner. There was no real evidence that he didn't, and he knew that husbands killed children too. More often their own. But not always.

CHAPTER 128

DI Chambers

Case reviews often moved the case forward. James always learned something new. Even if it was a new hypothesis that could be dismissed quickly as more evidence came to light. This case review was no different. There was plenty of new information to share. The attempted abduction of Holly had to be seen as likely to have been carried out by Charly and Samantha's killer. They couldn't call him a serial killer but no one in the room cared about this. Stanton wasn't a large city, it wasn't even a large town. It wasn't a village, but many residents had a village mentality. If you mentioned someone's name in a room of five people, chances are someone would know them. This killer was no doubt the worst and most prolific in Stanton's history. The entire police force and forensic community were determined to catch him whatever it took.

DI Chambers stood, and the room was silent. He began by reminding everyone that they could not jump to conclusions about any piece of evidence or any suspect. He reminded them about the interrogation of Josh Cummins and that just because he fulfilled two key pieces of the enquiry — working at Asda and attending Parks Mead School — this did not make him their killer. Although, there could well be others that shared the link, maybe more tenuously. For example, maybe they were unemployed but were regular shoppers in Asda or maybe they were friends with pupils that attended the school but went to the grammar school in the next town. There were still lines of enquiry to follow and they now needed to widen that net. He assigned particular officers to these tasks.

DS Khapor then stood. The attempted abduction of Holly Stretton was described in detail. A hand drawn map was included in everyone's packs alongside descriptions of both the attacker and his car. The attacker was wearing clothes which hid his identity but there were still descriptions of his height (5'11), possible weight (88kg) and skin colour (white IC1). He then asked a series of questions and made a number of statements. 'We know that the killer stalks his victims. We know that Nicole regularly shopped in Asda with the girls but where else did he stalk them? We need house to house in as wide an area as possible. We need forensics at any possible location that he could observe Holly from. The most obvious would be tall buildings. There are a number of flats in the vicinity. We need door to door there.'

One of the officers present laughed at this.

'We can ask residents in those flats whatever you like, they won't tell you anything,' he said.

'May I remind you that this is the attempted abduction of a young girl not a drugs bust. Make sure you state this at the start of each interview. There are many single parents and families living in those flats that will want the perpetrator caught as soon as possible,' DI Chambers said with authority.

DS Khapor continued. 'We need to find the make of car as quickly as possible. Nicole said it was light coloured and possibly a large four door. There must have been witnesses that saw it leave the area at speed. We need to find these.'

Then DS Khapor gave a list of team leaders for the house to house and gave out photocopies of the most important questions to ask.

Then it was the turn of forensics. Julie Smith, a forensic vehicle investigator, began. She was assertive and precise. She described what they had found with all three vehicles. She detailed the findings of the search of Mike Deyton's car. Everything was certain. There was no room for error. *The plastic bag must have snagged on the wheel rim as he loaded the body in the car.* This irritated James, but he kept his calm and tried to ignore it.

There was then a short comfort break. James was relieved, he needed to stretch his legs. He went over to the urn and poured himself a coffee. Rebecca Hastings, the forensic scientist, stood next to him. 'I could see you getting annoyed,' she whispered.

James said, 'When!'

'Julie is new. She's very strident. Isn't she. She's also very good at her job though. Very thorough. No one else would have found that piece of plastic. It was small and quite inaccessible. You should be glad we have her on our team,' Rebecca said.

James reminded himself that he should be more tolerant. He'd always been a logical, factual thinker. Facts had to be proven without doubt. That's why he'd always wanted to be a police officer. He thought that innocent until proven guilty was exactly that. He wouldn't tolerate error or arrogance from his officers, but this hadn't won him friends on the force. He questioned everything his colleagues did and often went over their work again. He was glad though that Rebecca, who he had the most time for, was reminding him of how he should not judge and dismiss others so easily.

'I'd better sort my papers. I'm up next,' Rebecca said breaking into his thoughts. She went to sit down but stopped and reached into her pocket for her phone. James noticed her smile as she looked at the screen.

A few minutes later, Rebecca was showing slides of the bag of tools that had been found a few days ago. She described the serrations on the knife and stated that it was extremely likely to be the murder weapon for Samantha's murder. The blood that had been found on the knife was a match to Samantha's DNA. She then showed pictures of the razor and stated that the tiny strands of blonde hair could not be used to extract DNA but were of the same or very similar colouring to Samantha's hair. She then turned from the slides to the room and said, 'We did find one other example of DNA. This was on the razor. It did not belong to Samantha. We ran it through the national database and we got a match within the last hour. His name is Ray Peterson. He was charged with assault five years ago. Assault against a prostitute.'

There was a sudden buzz of animated conversation in the room. DI Chambers stood up and asked for quiet. He then assigned a number of officers to particular roles. They needed to find out where Ray Peterson was living now and more about his previous assault.

CHAPTER 129

Sara

Sara hadn't been invited to the case review. She started her afternoon shift early. There were two lines of inquiry she was eager to follow. The first involved Tracey Munroe. A school friend had reminded her of the story of a bullied schoolboy who'd killed himself a number of year ago. They'd been a hanging on the local common and she'd remarked on how similar the previous case was. But it was the name of the schoolboy that had resonated — Robert Munroe. As soon as Sara had arrived at work, she'd put in a request for the paperwork. It couldn't just be a coincidence, surely.

While she waited for this, she returned to checking the names of all of the staff at Asda. It concerned her that that they hadn't done a complete history of all of the male workers. They had checked age and whether they had attended Parks Mead School but not work history. One person in particular bothered her. He was the trolley collector. She had a name but couldn't find any previous employment or addresses linked to that name. She had done searches on his date of birth but the only match she could find with the same name was for a boy that had died aged seven in a car accident.

DI Chambers hadn't returned by the time Sara was sent out on patrol. She decided that this information could wait until she finished her shift. By then she'd have more details about Robert Munroe.

CHAPTER 130

Emma

Emma and Nadiah met at Nadiah's house at 6am on Tuesday morning. Emma felt mildly excited. All she was going to do was knock his door, say "sorry, wrong house" and walk away. What could go wrong? She had changed so much since she'd last seen this guy. She had completely changed her hair colour from brown to pillar box red; changed her hairstyle from a bob to short and spiky. Even if he recognised the new Emma he wasn't likely to do anything in broad daylight.

They both decided to get it done as quickly as possible and they almost jogged to the trolley pusher's house. Nadiah stayed in the entry across the road. 'Don't worry I can see you from here,' she said. 'He can't see me though I checked the angle last night just to be sure. If anything happens, I will call the police.'

All the excitement had gone during the short walk. Emma now felt anxious. She almost decided to not go through with it. What was she thinking? This was madness.

Emma stepped out of the shadows, after getting a quick hug from Nadiah. After walking the short distance to the trolley pusher's front door, she knocked timidly and waited. Nothing happened. No one came. Then she knocked more firmly. She stepped back. Fearing the door would fly open and she would be faced by him. But no one came to the door. She didn't want to risk knocking again. She turned, walked down the path and crossed the road to Nadiah.

'He's not in.' Emma felt relieved. It had been a stupid idea.

'Maybe he doesn't answer the door to strangers. We could stay here a while. He might leave to go to work.' Nadia wrapped her jacket firmly around her.

Emma shuddered. 'Let's not. I'm not sure what good it will do. Even if he comes out, I won't get a clear view of him.'

CHAPTER 131

W

The Wig Maker was upstairs in the spare room when she knocked. He had decided to complete as much of the wig as he could from the final strands of Samantha's hair. When he heard the light knocking, he got up and moved the nets slightly to see outside. Just at that moment she had knocked again. Much harder this time and then she'd stepped back so he could see her properly. It was the lovely, delicious Emma. She had come to him.

Then she'd left. Running across the road to the entry opposite where she met someone with jet black hair. As this person turned towards him, he recognised her. It was Nadiah one of the cashiers from the shop. He'd often seen the two of them chatting. He didn't know they were friends though.

Now he was worried. What if they went to the police? He considered moving the wig and the equipment but where to? He needed it nearby. He would have to complete his final act quickly and soon. He resigned himself to never fully completing the wig. He gently combed it covering some of the bald patches. It was the exact colour he remembered. He moved it closer and smelled it. Them rubbed the side of his face against it. *Not long now,* he thought.

CHAPTER 132

Emma

Emma and Nadiah had gone back to Nadiah's house. They were sipping tea. Emma blew on hers. She liked her drinks piping hot. She always started drinking them as soon as the water was poured from the kettle but regretted it when they burned her mouth.

'What now?' asked Nadiah.

'I don't know it was probably a mad thing to do,' replied Emma.

'I could ring my supervisor and check when he's on shift. Then you could come into the supermarket and take another look at him.'

'Do you think I should contact Patrice or DI Chambers?'

'And say what? There's this odd trolley collector at Asda, he might be the killer. They would just pick him up, like Josh, and if it wasn't him, you'd feel so guilty,'

'But if it was, it might save a child's life.'

Emma ran her hand through her hair, so it stood up straight, lay back on Nadiah's sofa and stared at the ceiling. She'd ask Robert what he thought at visiting that afternoon. He would know what to do. She was missing him. The last couple of days had been hell. The first time they'd been apart in ages and certainly since Charly's death. All they'd done is go to work and then sit at home together barely speaking but she missed his presence. Missed his body warmth in bed. Missed his snoring even.

Nadiah interrupted he thoughts. 'Did you want some

breakfast?' she asked.

'No. It's fine. I'd better go home. I've got to go to the hospital later. Thanks though...' Emma got up off the sofa, hugged Nadiah and left.

CHAPTER 133

Nicole

Nicole had left Holly and Rosie with her neighbour, Sean, so she could attend the police station to look at possible pictures of Holly's abductor. It was either that or let them stay with one of the police officers. Sean had offered. He even came round to hers on the promise that he would ignore the mess.

She'd never been to a police station before. She walked up the steps leading to the front entrance with trepidation. She didn't want to see a picture of Holly's abductor. She knew if she recognised him that he was wanted for something else. She knew that he would be wanted for the murder of Charly Dean and Samantha Porter. Two girls aged six with long, blonde hair. Just like Holly. She promised her girls on the steps of the police station that no matter what essays she had to do, what work she might do in the future, they would always come first. She got to the top of the steps and pushed open the door to police reception.

As soon as she gave her name to the young police officer at reception she was led to an interview room. The room was cold and sparsely furnished, whilst she waited for DS Khapor she skimmed through the news pages on her phone. There had been no mention of Holly's attempted abduction in the news. The police had decided to keep it quiet. They had explained why but she hadn't really being listening. It was hard to concentrate at the moment.

DS Khapor entered the room five minutes later. He was carrying a tablet and a Manila folder. 'I just want you to look at a couple of photographs and sketches to help us with our enquiries,' he said.

He opened the tablet first. There were four sketches of a man with a weird hairline and centre parting. She stared at the hair not noticing his other features. The others were similar but had different hairstyles. 'Do you recognise this man?' DS Khapor asked.

'I'm not sure. I didn't see much of his face. Maybe if you covered the top of his face and from below his nose. DS Khapor did this electronically. Now Nicole could only see his eyes. She shuddered. 'I can't be certain, but they are the same shape.'

The face that Nicole saw when she closed her eyes. The face that tormented her. The hooded and masked face had eyes that were blank. The skin around them was barely lined. There was no puffiness that came with age. He looked young and yet his demeanour and gait made her think he was older. His skin had, also, been freckled and pale. She'd had the opportunity to notice that as she got closer and closer to him. Hitting him and pulling at Holly. She wanted to remember what he looked like even if it just the small part she could see.

DS Khapor then opened the manila folder and took out a number of photographs. He laid each of them on the table. These were of a number of men and were clearly taken in a police station. He asked Nicole to look carefully at each. She moved them as she looked. Dismissed them as not being relevant. She was left with one in front of her. He had the same eyes and this time she recognised the face. The hair was far less distinctive and he was far slenderer than he was now.

'I know him,' she simply said. 'He's the trolley guy at Asda. Oh god. That's why I feel uncomfortable in that shop. It's him isn't it and the eyes — it's him.'

She pushed away the photo and held on to the sides of the chair. DS Khapor immediately put the photographs back in the folder. He asked Nicole if she needed a cup of tea or a ride home. He couldn't get out of the room quick enough.

CHAPTER 134

Emma

Afternoon visiting hours were one until three. Emma followed the crowd to Robert's ward. They were all walking briskly not wanting to be the last ones in. Afraid that would make them look uncaring. All commenting on how hospitals made them feel and hoping that they wouldn't have to do this for much longer. All complaining about the cost of the car parking or the bus fare. About half of them used the hand wash dispenser on the wall before they went on the ward. Emma always did. She didn't want to add to Robert's woes by giving him MRSA or such like.

She entered the ward with the hustle and bustle of the queuing relatives and headed to Robert's bay. He was sitting up in bed. He'd been listening to music on his phone and he took off the headphones as she approached. She went over and kissed him. He winced. The bruises were coming out. His arms, legs and particularly his chest, or at least the area she could see that wasn't covered by the ridiculous pyjamas, were covered in bright purple, almost black bruises. He seemed happier though.

'Are my mum and dad not here?' he asked.

Emma muttered, 'No.'

'Good. I couldn't stand mum fussing any longer,' He took Emma's hand. 'I can't wait to come home. It's horrible not being home with you.'

Emma gave him a half smile and sat down on the plastic chair next to the bed. She'd decided on the way that she would tell him everything about her and Rich, and about the trolley pusher. The shock of his accident meant she wanted no more secrets.

She came right out and said it, 'I've seen Rich a few times on the boat.'

'He's your friend, Em. That's fine.' Robert didn't look concerned in fact he was smiling.

'I had a letter from someone. They put it in a book at the bookshop for me to find. It said that they were going to tell you I was having some kind of illicit affair with Rich.' Emma studied the patterns on the curtains at the side of Robert's bed. Too worried to look at Robert.

'You should have just told me, it's fine.' He was now brushing imaginary cotton off his sheets, not looking at Emma either.

Emma turned to look directly at Robert in his new pyjamas. He looked broken not strong. He never wore pyjamas in bed and she loved his muscular frame which was now discretely covered. She had to tell him everything. 'I thought about it. Thought about sailing away. Leaving Stanton and the grief behind…starting a new life…'

'With Rich.' Robert completed her sentence. 'You always loved him. I know that.'

'He's my best friend.'

'Shouldn't your husband be your best male friend.' Robert bit his lip.

Emma sensed that he regretted saying that, but in many ways it was true. In others it wasn't, she hadn't created a child with Rich. Her shared experiences with him were all fun and lighthearted. Her experiences with Robert were grown up and serious. Maybe Robert was her truest friend, after all. 'I just wanted to escape. It was foolish. I'm sorry.'

Sorry meant forgiveness. There was nothing to forgive, but the last thing Emma wanted was to hurt Robert.

'I found some hair.' It was Robert's turn to come clean. 'At Charly's grave, on her birthday…I found some blonde hair.'

Emma couldn't process this. Her mind twisted with the what ifs and whos and hows. It took her a while to respond.

'Why didn't you tell me?'

'I wanted to keep them in case they were Charly's. I knew you'd make me give them to the police.' He was looking down at the sheet again. His blonde lashes shielding his eyes. Emma stared at them, waiting for him to look round at her, knowing when he did that he'd look like a puppy that needed scolding.

Reality dawned. Emma was certain. 'He's been taunting us. The killer's been taunting us…I think I know who he is.'

'Em, what do you mean, you know who it is? Tell me. Tell me everything.'

It took her the rest of the visit to explain what had happened that morning. Robert kept interrupting wanting to know why she and Nadiah were being so stupid. Wanting to know why they thought it was him.

At the end of the visit Robert was silent. He seemed annoyed at her. They kissed but he seemed desperate for her to leave. She said she would see him at six that evening and he had just grunted.

CHAPTER 135

Robert

Robert couldn't believe what Emma had told him. The stuff about Rich, that was fine. That was expected. Rich was always there in the background. Emma's unfinished business. That's how he saw Rich. The one that sailed away. Robert knew why Rich went to Bristol. Why he left Stanton. It was because he loved Emma and couldn't stand the fact that she was with him instead. He'd left within months of them becoming a couple. If anything happened to Robert, then Rich would be there in a flash. He was sure of that. Rich would pick up the pieces and mend a broken Emma. So why had he chosen to come back now? That's what Robert didn't understand. But that wasn't what worried Robert the most. How could Emma and Nadiah be so stupid? Going to visit a possible killer while he sat here in this bed. He got up as soon as she left and went to the toilet. His legs were working fine. It was everywhere else that ached. His ribs, particularly, but he decided he could live with that.

He went to the nurse's station. One of the nurses was completing her notes. 'I want to discharge myself,' he said.

'The doctor will be around in an hour you can talk to her then,' the nurse said, without looking up from her notes.

'I want to discharge myself now,' Robert said more emphatically. He stopped holding his ribs too and tried to show that he was no longer in pain.

She looked up then and said, 'I can't advise that.'

'I don't need your advice. Just give me the forms to sign and some clothes. I don't know where mine are.'

'They were cut off you. You will have to wait for your wife to bring you some in.'

Robert looked down at his pyjamas and slippers. It would be worth the embarrassment to stop Emma doing anything stupid.

'I will leave like this…in a taxi. I'm sure they've seen worse.' he said.

The nurse got up and went to a filing cabinet. She gave Robert a number of forms and a pen.

'Here…make sure you read them. Contrary to what you may think we can't keep you here, but you need to be aware that it could make your health worse and you are leaving against medical advice. You may as well wait for the doctor though because it will take a few hours for your prescription to be ready.'

What could Emma do in a couple of hours? The pain was excruciating so he decided he had to wait for the painkillers at least. He didn't think he could get any that were as good as these over the counter. He signed the paperwork and went back to sit on the bed. He would wait for his prescription and leave.

CHAPTER 136

DI Chambers

It had been a busy day now they had a name. They had searched for Ray Peterson in every database they had. There was no record of him after his probation period had ended. No record of employment or on the electoral register. It was like he had vanished.

It was then James noticed that Sara was hovering at his door again. He was going to suggest that she apply to become a DC, but she really would need to be more assertive. He got up and opened the door. She visibly jumped as he did this.

'Sorry I was just about to knock,' she said.

He held the door open and she went to sit down. She sat with her hands tightly clasped as she spoke, 'Tracey Munroe had a brother called Robert. He committed suicide in 1996. I don't know how it is significant in this case but it's possibly relevant.'

DI Chambers pondered this. The Munroe family were clearly haunted by tragedy.

Sara still sat there, rubbing her hands together. 'Perhaps this is more important, I've found a discrepancy on the employment records at Asda.'

'Go on,' said James.

'The shopping trolley collector is using a false name. The name on his records is for a child that died in a car crash many years ago.' Sara said clearly and precisely.

At that moment DS Khapor entered James' office. He didn't knock. 'We've got a positive ID from Nicole. It's the trolley guy at Asda.'

Then everything happened at once. The Murder Investigation Team were brought together. Roles were assigned, risk assessments were written and issued, an arrest plan was drawn up and warrants were sought. All of this took time.

CHAPTER 137

W

The wig was as finished as it was ever going to be. He knew that. He'd need to act swiftly. He would wait until it was dark then act. He needed her alive that was the problem. How could he take her and where would they go? He'd bought drugs off the dark web that would keep her compliant and submissive. He'd always planned to keep her here and had set up a room to keep her in.

He left the third bedroom where he made the wig and entered the second bedroom at the back. Here was soundproofed walls, metal clasps and chains ground into the floor. There was even a bed which at some point he hoped to make use of. He'd always wanted to lose his virginity to Tracey. This had been a long time coming. Maybe he would have time to do that before they came for him. That was now his choice. Find a way to leave Stanton with Emma. Take all this with them. Find somewhere new to stay. Or snatch her now. Complete the transformation to Tracey. Maybe they would get one night or two together. They might not make the bed but he could show her how much he loved her with her chained to these walls if necessary. She would know then. Perhaps at that moment of climax he could kill them both. Slit her throat then his own.

He never normally allowed himself any comfort, any joy, but it seemed so close now. He put his hand down his trousers and began to pump his erect penis.

CHAPTER 138

Emma

Emma couldn't believe it. A taxi had pulled up outside and Robert got out in pyjamas and slippers. They couldn't have discharged him yet, surely. If they had, why hadn't they waited until she could bring him some clothes?

'I've discharged myself. We are going 'round there together. If it's him we will go straight to the police, I need it over,' Robert said as soon as she let him in.

'What do you mean?' Emma asked.

'This trolley guy. I need to know if it's him. You can show me the house and if it is him, either we can phone the police, or I'll sort it.'

Emma knew what sort it meant. She was completely torn on this. She wanted to see this guy even if it was to eliminate him as the killer, but she didn't want to go round there with Robert in this mood. He was in no fit state to become a vigilante avenger.

He'd gone upstairs though and was already getting dressed. She could hear him grimacing at each movement as he put on his clothes.

He came back downstairs a few minutes later. He went to get the helmets. He gave Emma hers. 'Here,' he said. 'You can show me where this bastard lives.'

Choice time. Emma took the helmet and went to find her leather jacket.

When they were riding to the trolley pusher's house Emma decided that she would just knock the door again. She'd make Robert stay in the place Nadiah had hidden and then he could call the police if anything happened. That would be the safest option. She would only need to see his whole face then she would know.

The ride there was too quick. She'd tapped Robert on the shoulder every time he needed to make a right or left turn and now they were here at the house. Emma felt far more apprehensive having Robert here than she had that morning with Nadiah. You would have thought that being here with a young woman would have been scarier than with a grown man, but it wasn't. This morning had been a bit of an adventure. It had seemed quite simple. A knock and run. But Emma didn't know what Robert would do if she recognised this guy. He'd probably kill him or at least try to. As she got off the bike, she had an even worst thought. This could be the place where her daughter was murdered, where she took her last breath.

CHAPTER 139

DI Chambers

DS Chambers was waiting for the warrant to search Ray Peterson's house to be agreed. As soon as they had that they were leaving. There were officers ready in two vans. They had all been fully briefed. Ray wasn't working today. They expected, but couldn't be certain, that he was at home.

He hoped this was it. If it was then instead of simply putting money behind the bar for his officers to have a drink on him, he would actually join them. This man needed to be caught. For once he was certain. There was enough evidence to charge him. He'd made a list.

Ray Peterson had previously served a prison sentence of six months for assaulting a prostitute. The prostitute's name was Shana Taylor. She had brassy blonde hair and described Ray as a stalker who followed her around and had never been a client. He gave her the creeps. On the night of December 2nd, 2014, he had grabbed Shana around the neck as she was leaving an alleyway to return to her patch. She'd managed to escape his grip and had reported him to the police station the next morning,

Ray Peterson attended Parks Mead School and was in the same year as Tracey Munroe,

Ray Peterson used a false name while working as a trolley collector at Asda.

Ray Peterson's blood was found on the razor blade used to shave Samantha Dean's hair.

Ray Peterson was positively identified as the man who tried to abduct Holly Stretton.

Even the Crown Prosecution Service would see that this was enough to charge Ray Peterson. DS Chambers was sure of this. Now all the needed was that warrant.

CHAPTER 140

Emma

Emma knocked on the door and waited. It opened almost immediately. They guy that stood in front of her was the trolley collector. He was, also, the man in the bookshop. DS Chambers had been right, he'd worn a wig that day. Now he looked as near to normal as anyone could.

Before she could say that she had knocked the door at the wrong house, the man spoke, 'Hello, Emma. I've been wanting to talk to you for a long time. To explain.'

Emma couldn't move. She wanted to run but felt rooted to the ground. He wasn't touching her but she felt his grip tighten around her. He stared at her and smiled.

'There's nothing to be afraid of. I just want to explain why I did it.'

He had a soft, imploring voice. Monotone. Almost hypnotic. Not what she'd been expecting at all. She almost wanted to listen to what he had to say. She certainly couldn't speak or move. He took her arm and led her into the house. She knew she should fight. Run away back to Robert, but she couldn't. She wanted to know why. She'd always wanted to know why.

The front door shut behind them. He led her upstairs and she didn't protest. It was only when they entered the spare bedroom and she saw the chains and arm locks that she tried to escape. His grip was strong on her arm. The more she struggled, the tighter it got. She had completely misjudged his size and strength. Instead of locking her up, he sat her down on the only chair. 'Stay there,' he demanded.

She did as she was told.

He locked the door with a key and sat on the bed.

'I can chain you up if you like,' he said. 'But I think you want to hear what I have to say.'

She didn't speak or move. She sat transfixed.

'You left me before I had the chance to tell you what I felt. You were too good for them. They had no clue what you were. I would have treated you better. You could have lived however you wished and wherever you wished. I would never have left you. Never have used you.'

Emma realised he wasn't talking about her or Charly. He was talking about that other girl, Tracey,

'I can help,' she simply said. Not even sure why she said it. It's what she always said. Always the peace maker. Always trying to make things better. But not this. Surely not this.

'You have to understand that I did it because I had to. I needed the hair you see. Without the hair none of this would work. Robert needed to pay. He used you and cast you aside. But Emma...' he stopped speaking and looked directly at her. His voice becoming more menacing. 'Emma...your hair is the wrong colour and thickness. Everything else would work, but not your hair.'

Emma tried to move then. Fear and adrenaline suddenly taking over. He'd expected this. He grabbed at her arms and forced her back into the chair.

At the same moment, they both heard the glass breaking downstairs.

Emma was pushed aside, knocked to the floor, as he unlocked the door and went in search of whoever was breaking in. He had the foresight to lock the door behind him.

Emma sat staring at the door. For a moment unable to move, like a frightened rabbit on a country road. She knew she had to take stock of her situation. Looking around, she hoped to discover a weapon. The room was bare. Apart from the bed and the chains, there was nothing. Even a search under the bed found nothing, not even dust.

CHAPTER 141

Robert

Robert couldn't believe Emma had gone into the house how could she have been so stupid. This guy hadn't even had to force her. She'd just walked in. He had dialled 999. Then he'd hung up before anyone answered. What would he say? His wife had gone into a house with a man they didn't know? They wouldn't come for that. If he had to explain who he and Emma was and that they thought this man had killed their daughter, it might be too late for Emma. He had to find a way in there. Fast.

He went around the back. Hoping that the back door might be unlocked, when he got there, he realised that if he broke in then the neighbours would phone the police, which would be a good thing. He found a brick and threw it through the kitchen door window. The key was in the lock inside, he tried to turn it, but his arm was at an awkward angle. He found another brick and used it to knock more of the glass out. His hand slipped through the hole, he turned the key in the lock and walked in.

He was confronted by a man whom he vaguely recognised. Before he could guess who it was, he spied the knife he confidently held in front of him. The man plunged the serrated blade at Robert, who wasn't quick enough to step away. It penetrated his jacket and pierced the skin between his ribs. The pain was excruciating. Robert stumbled and hit his head on the edge of the sink as he fell. He didn't feel anything more.

CHAPTER 142

DI Chambers

DI Chambers and the arrest team were heading to Ray Peterson's address when the call came through. There had been a possible burglary reported by a neighbour at that same address, twenty minutes ago. They were at least ten minutes away. He told the driver to speed up.

He didn't know who was breaking in or why it had taken so long for dispatch to let them know about the call. Heads would roll for that. He just hoped they weren't too late. Many different scenarios passed through his mind. None of them good. Most of them involving vigilante husbands and fathers putting their lives at risk.

CHAPTER 143

W

The Wig Maker knew he didn't have long. He went to fetch the wig from the third bedroom. He inspected it as he took it off the dummy head. He smelled it. It was the finest, softest human hair. You couldn't buy this anywhere. He felt a sense of pride and excitement. He had achieved what he had set out to do. Tracey had come to him.

He went to her. Unlocked the door and now all she needed was to be dressed. She had shrunk. Her back was pressed against the wall away from him. Her legs were pulled up and she was hugging her knees. He should shackle her, but he needed this to be quick. Putting the wig on the bed, he took the knife out of the back pocket of his jeans and made sure that she could see it was wet with blood. Then, he placed that within reach on the bed, next to the wig.

He moved towards Tracey, placing the wig carefully on her head and the transformation was complete. He licked her face and then pushed his tongue inside her mouth. Only briefly so she wouldn't bite it. He now had one of his knees between her legs and pressed against her stomach, so she couldn't move. One of his hands held her wrists together. The other reached for the knife. 'I will kill you,' he said.

CHAPTER 144

Robert

Robert opened his eyes. The light hurt. In fact, everything hurt, he closed them again. Then he realised where he was and what had happened. He forced himself up. He was bleeding but not badly. His leather jacket had stopped the knife from completely penetrating his skin and lung.

He tried to stand. This winded him and he leant against the sink for a moment struggling to breathe. He had to get to Emma. He stumbled and dragged himself through to the living room and then heard a thump from upstairs. He went into the hall, grabbed the stair rail and hauled himself up the stairs. Ignoring the pain, he had to save Emma.

Some element of surprise was essential, so he entered the front bedrooms as quietly as he could. The first looked like an average bedroom. Tidier than most. There was no Emma. He moved on. The second had just a dressing table in it with a number of tools neatly laid out on a roll of cloth. He picked up a hammer and moved on to the next.

He opened the door as quietly as he could. Emma was forced against the back wall. She was wearing a blonde wig which had fallen askew. The man had his knee forcing her legs apart. He was about to undo the zip on her jeans.

Robert raised the hammer. The man must have heard him. He turned as quickly as he could and slashed at Robert with the knife. Robert stepped backwards to escape the blade. He tripped and fell to the floor.

CHAPTER 145

Emma

Emma had been ready to give up. In her head she was ready to meet Charly. She didn't care what this man did to her. It was over. He could rape her if he wished. She had gone to a better place.

But then she saw Robert in the doorway with a hammer raised and everything changed. She could live. She could defeat this monster. The man must have sensed this and turned in time to slash at Robert. As she saw Robert fall. She found new strength. She was Charly's Bat Girl. The avenger for justice. She jumped on the man's back and pushed her finger into one of his eyes. She felt him squirm beneath her. He still had the knife which he was waving about trying to reach her arms. She grabbed his arm and whacked it with as much force as she could against the wall. The knife fell from his grasp. Before he could drop to the floor. She pushed herself away from him, knelt down and reached for the knife. As he turned, she lunged at him. The knife entered between his ribs. The force upward into his chest.

It took what seemed like minutes for him to fall. Robert had got to her in that time. He took the knife off her and stabbed him too. Then dropped the knife and held her.

CHAPTER 146

DI Chambers

DI Chambers arrived at the house of Ray Paterson after 6pm. The back door had been broken into and the officers entered unimpaired. There was a pool of blood on the kitchen floor and two bricks which had been used to break the glass in the door.

The parade of police searched the downstairs before proceeding up the stairs. There was blood on the handrail.

They found Emma and Robert still holding on to each other. Ray Peterson lay dead at their feet. Blood from two knife wounds pooled beneath him. As James led Robert and Emma out of the room. He spotted Robert's knife wound and he radioed for an ambulance. They were clearly both in shock. James carefully removed the wig from Emma's hair for some reason he muttered, 'That's better.'

The time for interviews would come later. The parents were safe. The killer was dead that was all that mattered. There was, however, a scene to protect and the immediacy of this took over. Everyone left the house and waited for the forensic team. He put Emma and Robert in a police car to wait for the ambulance. They were hugging each other still. James remembered how far apart these parents had been when he first met them.

CHAPTER 147

Emma

It had been six months since Emma had killed her daughter's murderer. She still sometimes felt the knife in her hand. She tried to move on, but it was hard. How do you work in a bookshop knowing you have stabbed someone in the heart? All of those crime fiction books could be about you.

She lay on the bed in Charly's room. They were going to move the bed out later that day. She stroked her stomach and looked up at the ceiling. 'I'm sorry, Charly.' She said. 'You will never meet your new brother or sister. I hope you don't mind if we redecorate your room. What do you reckon? A sunny yellow? Maybe we will change it later when we know what we are having.'

She would keep all of Charly's clothes and toys in the loft in boxes. She couldn't give them away. She couldn't see them being played with either. Most of her things were now packed away. It was just the bed which would be replaced with a cot.

But, of course, Charly could never be replaced. Emma lay there and surrounded herself with all the moments they had shared. Blocking all the images of death and murder with images of Charly playing, climbing trees and swinging as high as she could. Her Bat Girl doll beside her.

CHAPTER 148

Robert

Robert cleaned his bike. Polished it until it sparkled. He'd told Emma that he was getting it ready to sell. But this wasn't exactly true. He was getting it ready to trade in for a newer model. Maybe a cruiser or a naked street bike. He hadn't made up his mind.

His role was as protector and here he was contemplating buying another bike to race the wind on. The last year had taught him that you can survive a tragedy. You can move forward. It won't make you a better person, just a different one. He hadn't been able to protect Charly from the evil in the world. But he would do everything in his power to protect the new baby.

Emma hadn't told him that she had stopped taking the pill. He could have considered this a betrayal, but he didn't. He understood her need to nurture and love a child. To be truthful, he'd felt the same. Fear had stopped him raising the idea. Fear that they were no longer close as a couple. That their relationship had too many chips around the edge and hairline cracks to withstand a return to parenthood. When Emma had told him that she was pregnant, he had picked her up like a doll, held her close and cried. Even the thought of that day made him well up. Nothing felt more right.

It masked the horror of the previous nine months. He didn't see that evil bastard's face every time he shut his eyes. He no longer replayed his perceived vision of Charly's murder on a loop.

Previously knowing who had committed the murder only sharpened the focus, making it more vivid. It didn't even help that he'd slid a knife up to the hilt into the killer's heart. It made no difference at all. That had left him numb. He understood how soldiers felt. If you have enough hate in you then you cannot mourn a death at your own hands. It simply becomes a necessary action. Maybe it would hit him at some point.

Now, he had one purpose. He had to keep Emma and the new baby safe. Emma wouldn't let him wrap them both in cotton wool. But he'd be a watchful eye from a careful distance. Always ready to pick them up when they fell. Always ready to protect them from the monsters. When the time was right, he'd hand Charly's Bat Girl toy on to this child and send them out to face the world.

Printed in Poland
by Amazon Fulfillment
Poland Sp. z o.o., Wrocław